"I would never purposefully hurt you," he said. **"But it is my nature. I need blood to survive."**

"I understand."

"Do you?" He clenched a fist, then opened it, studying the brief red imprints his nails had left in the palm. "*Why* do you? Who are you? What are you?"

The woman should be ranting, screaming, cringing at the insanity of finding a vampire sharing the same home with her.

"What's wrong, Jane? Scared of me?"

"I don't fear a man who cannot understand his own nature." She touched his cheek, and it was so gentle, too soft, that Michael flinched. "You don't know how to control it, do you? That's why you're here. You're not exhausted, you're hiding from the blood hunger."

MICHELE HAUF

When polling her friends, they will generally report that Michele Hauf is the weird one. But then, *weird* doesn't quite define her either—more like *different*.

Her interests range from flamenco music, to heavy metal, to soundtracks (most especially *Chitty Chitty Bang Bang*). Her spare time is spent perusing and shellacking rocks, decorating dragonflies, and thinking about France and when, exactly, she was a musketeer (and was that the Black or Gray regiment?). Toss in a fascination for the art nouveau time period and season it with chocolate, dumplings and gallons of Orangina. Faeries and cats are also always welcome, as well as vampires, crosses, glass doorknobs and any kind of high-tech gadget. Yeah, *different* is good.

Michele has been writing for over a decade and has published historical, fantasy and paranormal romance. She lives with her family in Minnesota, and loves the four seasons, even if one of them lasts six months and can be colder than a deep freeze. You can find out more about her at www.michelehauf.com.

MICHELE HAUF

FROM THE DARK

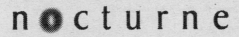

Silhouette Books

nocturne

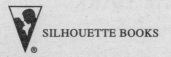 **SILHOUETTE BOOKS**
®

ISBN-13: 978-0-373-61750-0
ISBN-10:   0-373-61750-X

FROM THE DARK

Copyright © 2006 by Michele Hauf

All rights reserved. Except for use in any review, the reproduction or utilization of this work in whole or in part in any form by any electronic, mechanical or other means, now known or hereafter invented, including xerography, photocopying and recording, or in any information storage or retrieval system, is forbidden without the written permission of the editorial office, Silhouette Books, 233 Broadway, New York, NY 10279 U.S.A.

All characters in this book have no existence outside the imagination of the author and have no relation whatsoever to anyone bearing the same name or names. They are not even distantly inspired by any individual known or unknown to the author, and all incidents are pure invention.

This edition published by arrangement with Harlequin Books S.A.

® and TM are trademarks of Harlequin Books S.A., used under license. Trademarks indicated with ® are registered in the United States Patent and Trademark Office, the Canadian Trade Marks Office and in other countries.

Visit Silhouette Books at www.eHarlequin.com

Printed in U.S.A.

Dear Reader,

What is the attraction to vampires? Over the past ten years the amount of vampire romances published has increased tenfold. Isn't that incredible? I, for one, am very glad they continue to be so popular.

Of course, it is their dark, forbidden appeal that draws me. And if the vampire is also a rock star—yet another appealing bad-boy image—then the attraction is doubled. Michael Lynsay is a shy, sweet young man eager to follow his rock-and-roll dreams. But fame, fortune and vampirism—all at one time—is a lot to deal with. I needed to explore Michael's life, and discover how he would deal with all that. And who, exactly, would counter his fall to the dark side? Simple, but mysterious, Jane offered to take the challenge. Together, they both hold secrets detrimental to the other. But the fun part was figuring a way to bring them together, no matter the odds.

I hope you enjoy Michael's story. I know he'll live forever in my heart.

Michele Hauf

To all the fans of *Dark Rapture* who have written me over the years. It's been a while, but the vamps are back. I hope Michael and Jane mean as much to you as Sebastian and Scarlet do.

Acknowledgments

Special thanks to Tara Gavin for inviting me to write for Nocturne. What an opportunity to get back to the vampires I love!

Appreciation goes to Sean Mackiewicz, Charles Griemsman and Adam Wilson, editorial assistants extraordinaire, who never cease to amaze me with their dedication to the stories that must cross their desks by the multitudes. You guys rock!

Thank you to Mary-Theresa Hussey, who took a chance on me years ago when LUNA was debuting. Since then, she's gotten me involved with the Bombshell line, a deliciously fun series to write for.

The Harlequin/Silhouette art department is another amazing bunch. The cover faeries have been very, very good to me. Thank you!

Maureen Stead, in Publicity and Promotion, you're a peach.

I must admit I am addicted, not only to the wonderful writing opportunities available at Harlequin, but to the generous personalities I have had the pleasure to work with over the phone, via e-mail and on the written page. Thank you all!

Chapter 1

Count seven tombstones to the left, and then, five tombstones up. A pair of dark eyes observed him from behind a paperback book. Her attire, entirely black, matched fingernails, eye shadow and hair.

Sunglasses propped at the end of his nose, Michael averted his eyes from the woman's morbid curiosity. In his hands, he held an iPod. The screen played The Fallen's next video, *Pieces of Rapture*. The final cut looked awesome. He switched it off, tugged the earbuds from his ears, and tucked the slim white player into his back pocket.

"What do you think?" he said as he squatted before a granite tombstone that glittered with chunks of mica. "Not bad for a small-town Minnesota boy, eh?"

The graveyard was quiet this evening, the humidity of summer pushing away spring with a burst of warm wind through Michael's hair. Three hundred twenty-seven tombstones were arrayed around him. Two rusted shovels leaned against the chain-link fence to the north. One brick shed must store grounds-keeping supplies.

The goth chick still studied him from behind cover. Michael waved, acknowledging her. She sneered, and flipped him off.

"Whatever happened to Minnesota nice?" he muttered.

Probably went the same way his *nice* had gone. The real world offered so much in way of temptation and addictions. How desperately he held on to any remnants of humanity still within him.

He rested the heel of his hand upon the curved top of the tombstone and, with his other hand, traced a forefinger through the words carved into the stone. Shards of wilted grass blades sifted to the freshly mown lawn. Noting the brass vase stabbed into the ground at the base of the tombstone, Michael winced. He should have brought flowers. She deserved flowers by the armload.

"Been a while since I've come home." He scanned the sky through the dark sunglasses. The sun had just set. Remnants of rose-colored warmth traced the horizon. "Our band is at the top of its game. We played at the Grammies this year. The press has dubbed us a phenomenon. And guess what? It's my birthday in a few weeks. We'll celebrate together. Life is good, Mom. I certainly have nothing to complain about."

No, no complaints. And yet, the monster within him growled a protest or two.

On the outside, Michael Lynsay wore a mask for the world to scream at. And man, did they scream. Loud, wild, rock 'n' roll screams of joy.

He liked the screams. Life, in general, was all about the scream. And him? Master of screams. For with the scream, came the delicious adrenaline, and that was an exquisite drug.

Michael had achieved success by going for it, and by reaching for a dream. And though the dream stomped him daily, he continued to soar on the incredible highs it also offered. Rock star, anyone? A man couldn't ask for a better gig.

But beyond the adulation of screaming fans, lurked an unforgiving, hungry monster, that would not take no for an answer.

Sooner or later the spotlight would shine upon that creature, and then Michael would be forced to flee even deeper into the darkness that shrouded his life.

Tugging the music rag from his back jeans pocket, Michael unrolled the tightly twisted newspaper he'd picked up after landing at the Minneapolis-St. Paul International airport an hour earlier. The headline made him smirk. *Fallen Angel sets down his microphone. Rumored exhaustion.*

Fallen Angel is what the fans had dubbed him, because reporters were always comparing his voice to that of a fallen angel screaming back at Heaven.

But exhaustion? That's what he paid the band's spin doctors for—lies.

Thing is, he had never felt so alive in his entire life. Frenetic and bold, he had become something different. A something he had learned to embrace.

Now, it was threatening to consume him. He had to keep his head above the surface. Out of the dark.

On more than one occasion, he'd almost exposed his darkest secret in public. The press followed him everywhere. They made it difficult to take a piss in private, let alone find a moment of peace to feed his habit.

Michael's best friend, Jesse Olson, the band's lead guitarist, had finally convinced Michael to step down from the stage, for a few months at the very least.

"I don't know if this is the right thing. I'm going to be missing out on—"

"On absolutely nothing." Jesse had placed a palm to each of Michael's shoulders and eyed his friend squarely. "Listen, man, The Fallen has been on the road for a year. Steady. No breaks. The new album is in the can and the video is going to be hot. We all need a vacation, Michael. After the MTV thing this Friday, me and the rest of the guys are a few days behind you."

"I don't need a vacation."

"That's what you think. And—" Jesse rushed in before Michael could protest "—you will take it. I don't want to lose you, man. You're my best friend. Even if you are a bloodsucker."

"Settle down, Jesse, I'm not going anywhere."

"Your mind may not be, but it's your soul I'm worried about, Michael." He slapped a hand over Michael's heart, and the singer clasped Jesse's wrist.

They both knew what Jesse hadn't been able to voice. Michael was so close to losing control. And if he did? There was no going back.

Jesse had offered Michael the house he'd purchased a year ago, and—since it was private property—had given him permission to enter and use the place as he wished, for however long it took.

How long did it require to kick a habit? A deadly habit.

"A few months' exile in an empty estate in rural Minnesota," Michael said now. "It's been a while since I've been back. Seem to remember gas being less than a dollar then. And no one had even heard of MTV."

He'd grown up in North Lake and would never tire of the small-town hominess and quiet goodness of the people. Hell, after doing the tour bus for over a year, he craved the rustic charm that reminded him of his childhood—creepy goth chick not included. And it wasn't as though he couldn't afford the missed time. He'd made himself a pretty penny over the past few years, and, like Jesse, had an excellent investment manager.

Michael stood. "If I don't do this," he said to his mother's grave, "I will lose my career. And if that's not bad enough, I risk loss of humanity. I just want… I don't want to lose it. I won't step over that edge. A line must be drawn. Some things in this world are not acceptable."

Like murder.

But he was close. Michael walked a fine line between taking what he needed, and taking everything.

Behind him a familiar *chirr* stirred the air. Michael swung about. His senses honed on the swish of maple leaves, and the scamper of squirrels nearby on the grass. He scanned the hedgerows; high as his shoulders, they blocked out the lazy city street on the other side. Many old, wide oaks—which a person could easily hide behind—dotted the graveyard.

Sniffing the air, he sought the scent of an intruder. Acrid and stale, fear scent was easy to pinpoint. And yet, he scented nothing inordinate beyond the black nail polish the goth chick must use by the gallons.

He knew that sound. A man didn't spend years of his life on the road playing gigs at every major stadium without running into the paparazzi daily, and learning to loathe them.

Fists forming at his sides, Michael clenched his jaw. "You bastards have no right!"

To follow him here? To interrupt while he took a few moments with his dead mother?

A glance to the goth chick found her poring over the book. Michael swung his shoulders to scan the periphery. He avoided noting the inscriptions on the tombstones—some were beautifully decorated with crosses and heartfelt quotes.

Chains strapped around the ankles of his leather boots clinked out his anger as Michael stomped across the cemetery plots. A shadow danced across the brick wall siding the north end of the grave-yard. He rushed toward the utility shed and gripped the neck of the shadow, shoving it against the wall.

"Where's the camera?" Michael demanded.

He slammed his palm against the guy's shoulder. His catch was small and squirmy, a mere teenager. "In your pocket?"

"I don't have one! You're hurting me!"

"Man, this isn't a hurt, you'll know a hurt when I give it. Empty your pockets. Can't a guy have one moment of peace?"

"Y-you're a public figure."

"Yeah, and you bastards hound me every step I take. Is it too much to ask that when I stop to visit my dead mother, I can get some private time?"

"I didn't take p-pictures. Honest."

"Then what are you doing here? Who are you? I know you've been following me. The cab driver pointed out the same yellow VW every time we turned."

Michael shoved hard against the boy's shoulder. He could break bones with ease, but he had no intention of causing harm, just frightening him.

"Ouch! I have been following you. You're famous, Mr. Lynsay. I just wanted to look—"

"Camera?"

"My camera is in the car."

Dropping the kid like a sizzling coal, Michael then stepped back as if he were skipping away from rising flames. Now the boy's fear scent invaded his nostrils. Michael feared nothing—except himself.

It was the fear he found in others—mortals—that drew him, for it was always laced with adrenaline.

A rich aroma wavered into his body, tickling his blood. Awakening—

They were not alone. Michael switched his sensory focus to his surroundings. Avoid a scene, at all costs. Especially with a witness nearby.

After The Fallen's first appearance on MTV, Michael had accepted the lack of privacy that accompanied fame. Females rushed him. Men sang his songs at the sight of him. Reporters were constantly trying to find out whom he was dating. Paparazzi were part of the daily routine. But when they intruded on personal moments, then he had to draw the line.

"Bring the camera to me."

"I haven't taken any pictures." His hands shaking, the kid swiped at a stream of sweat above his brow. "Not yet."

His fear had settled. He told the truth.

The rags paid top dollar for exclusive pictures. Michael could imagine what a shot of him in a graveyard would go for. More than he raked in for a week's worth of concerts, no doubt.

"Get out of here."

The kid stood there, stubbornly lifting his jaw, so Michael snarled and made a false lunge for him. That got his feet scissoring swiftly out of the gated graveyard. "Thanks for nothing!" he hollered back.

Swiping a hand down his face, Michael gave one last glance around the graveyard. The goth chick had split.

Jesse was right. He did need this self-imposed exile. A break from situations like what had just occurred. To put it bluntly? A break from people, which would then allow him the opportunity to fight the addiction to their fear.

Truth be told, he could not survive without people; they had become both bane and boon to his life.

This was going to be tough. Was he ready?

Exile. Michael exhaled. The concept didn't fit his idea of a good time.

Perhaps one last fix before he locked himself away?

"Most definitely," he muttered.

Chapter 2

A slice of Decadent Darkness sat across the table from Jane Rénan. The chocolate layers taunted her mercilessly as her friend shoveled the dessert into her mouth. A plain piece of apple pie sat untouched before Jane, already cooled. Extremely jet-lagged after the flight from Venice to the States, she looked forward to sleep.

"You're staying at a hotel tonight?" Ravin Crosse asked around a forkload of creamy chocolate ganache. "Why don't you go right to the house?"

Ravin always said exactly what was on her mind.

"It's late, and I'm tired. I've never been to the house, so I guess I prefer meeting it for the first time in the daylight."

"You're not weird about the night, are you?" Ravin's dark brow quirked, another forkful of chocolate hung suspended before her lips. "I know you're not afraid of the creepies, Jane. So what gives?"

"I'm not afraid, and I don't expect any creepies," Jane defended wearily. She caught her chin in hand and tried to keep from collapsing in her pie. "Seriously, I need sleep. Now."

"North Lake is a good hour drive from here. I plan on heading up that way after we're done. If you don't mind sitting on the chopper, I can give you a lift."

"Ravin, I've just done three countries in two days, overseeing installations for clients. Can I please just get some room service and a mint on my pillow tonight? Besides, I don't do motorcycles."

"Street chopper," Ravin correctly with a pirate grin that glittered in her dark eyes.

Jane had been pleased that Ravin was able to meet her on such short notice, and that she'd easily agreed to help her locate a source. "The moon is full in two weeks. I know that doesn't give you much time."

"Don't worry, I've got the Sight."

"You do?" Aware of the half-dozen late night patrons positioned close by, Jane leaned across the table to whisper. "But—doesn't that come at a steep price?"

Scraping up the last traces of sweetness, Ravin then cleaned the fork with a satisfied purr. "Not my soul, if that's what you're thinking."

She *had* been thinking that. The Sight did not

come cheaply, and it was rumored, sparely doled out—and not by just anyone, but by *Himself.*

Ravin tugged up her black T-shirt to just below her breasts, and in the dank light of the café, displayed the price she had paid. Three vertically stacked horizontal lines were carved into her flesh. The wounds looked fresh. Jane knew they would remain so.

"Three strikes and I'm out," Ravin offered with little emotion, and a tight smirk. She tugged her shirt down. "But it's worth it. I can see them now, Jane. No more mistakes. Sighting in a source for you will be like snapping bees off the flower. Not that they've been prancing the streets out in the open much lately. The tribes have gone to ground thanks to an insurgence of werewolves in the city."

"That's not good."

"No, but because of that, many are spreading out through the suburbs. Don't worry. I'll find you a source before the full moon. It's what I do."

"And you are the best." Relieved, Jane dug into her pie. With Ravin on her side, she had little to worry about now, except preparing herself for the rest of her life.

Leaving the edge of darkness, Michael's sight skipped over the alleyway's sparkling pools of grimy water, then wavered and refocused. A woman's face stared up at him, teasing him with her lost life.

Was she really—?

His breaths huffed out abruptly. He couldn't have

gone that far. Well, he could have—but, no. He hadn't.

"Don't be dead," he hissed. "I can't succumb to this. It's…damn it! It is too difficult to stop!"

Paralleling her face with a palm, he stroked the air, not daring to touch her skin. Her blonde hair swirled in a puddle left over from this afternoon's rain. Streetlights glittered in her staring green eyes. *I shall haunt you in your dreams.*

If he had indeed killed, the nightmares would come, for a kill would draw his victim's nightmares into his soul for the final danse macabre.

There wasn't anything taboo about the kill; others of his kind did it frequently, and, he had come to learn, without regret. It was an innate need pushed to the extreme. But Michael's aversion to the act had become his greatest bane. He wasn't like the others. He didn't want to become a killer. He didn't *need* to kill. But the addiction was merciless.

"Have I really done it?"

So easy to make the kill. You can do it, Michael. Such unholy bliss can be yours. Just…take it.

He'd vowed to never kill. He was better than that. He tried to be better.

Had the monster won this time?

"Please, don't be dead."

Kneeling, his hand resting upon his knee, Michael searched the woman's eyes even as the last traces of her blood slithered down the back of his throat. Was there life in there?

Seeking escape from her silent accusation, he looked up to the midnight sky. Easier to see the stars out here at the edge of the suburbs, than in the city, but still so little light up there.

Cars drove by in the distance, the tires spitting up water in their wake. The trance beat from the Decadance club echoed out to where he knelt, tucked deep in an alley where there were no windows. Ten paces away a smelly garbage can curdled the air. The lake lay but two blocks to the east and the keen of a gull taunted him from overhead.

He traced a finger down her arm and over the tangle of silver, gold and rubber bracelets on her wrist. Seven in all. One pink silicone band stood out.

Mortal diseases couldn't touch him. But that didn't mean he couldn't be touched by a human's destruction.

She was most valiant in her fight to the end.

The doctor's words, spoken so long ago, still haunted Michael. His mother had bravely battled breast cancer for years. Modern medicine had come so far since then.

But no regrets. He tapped the thin silver band he wore on his left wrist. His mother's. Truly, she had lived as valiantly as she had died.

And what would she think of the monster he had become?

You shouldn't be here. You're stronger than this.

Exactly.

The scent of blood suddenly sickened Michael. He

felt his gorge heat the back of his throat. Garbage stench entered his pores. He couldn't scrub away the crime.

Breathing deeply, Michael stared at the creep of crimson purling from the woman's neck. The vein pulsed. *Still alive.* He'd not taken much. Only what was necessary.

Was his monster's necessity a crime?

No. He'd not killed. Murder wasn't in his arsenal. He was still Michael Lynsay from North Lake, Minnesota, boy-wonder-singer, and a mean right arm with the snowballs. He'd taken first place in the 4-H horticultural competition his senior year. That same year he'd almost been crowned homecoming king until the queen had found out he'd slept with her best friend. He loved his mother—God rest her soul—and he used to go to church every Sunday. So very, very long ago.

Michael Lynsay still lived—*somewhere*—within this vampire.

Reaching to stroke the blond hair, he stopped. *Leave no trace.*

Drawing his tongue across his fingertips, he wetted them and then smeared his saliva over the double puncture wounds. And then he leaped up and took off in a stride, turning sharply down another alleyway.

He didn't get far. An arrogant shadow stood in the middle of the alley, arms akimbo and head cocked at an accusatory angle. The spare moonlight avoided her.

It was a woman, short and slender, dressed in dark clothing and not at all unattractive. He wasn't

far from the club. If he could get by with an autograph then he could be on his way. But as he neared
her, he recognized the pale, grinning face beneath the
sweep of black hair.

"You lost?" she asked on a sharp hiss.

Michael backed away at sight of the huge silver
cross suspended around her neck. The thing had to
weigh a pound and it captured the streetlight in so
many wicked sparkles.

"You look familiar," he said, trying to act nonchalant and not cringe at the cross. "And I should be
asking you the same. The club is that way."

"Don't dance. And neither do you, unless it's a
danse macabre, eh?"

She had seen. She *knew.*

"What are you talking about, lady?" He smoothed
a hand over his chest, lifting his shoulders. Not a
man to be messed with. Nor a creature she wanted
to piss off. "If you were spying on me and the chick
making out, sorry, I'm all tapped out tonight."

"Making out? Is that what you call it? I wouldn't
touch you if I was wearing a haz-mat suit." She paced
around him, keeping them at a good eight feet apart.

It was the woman he'd seen in the graveyard.
But this was no depressed, pale goth chick seeking
the strange. This woman looked wired, ready and
dangerous.

"How long you in town for, big boy?"

Squaring his shoulders and hooking his thumbs
in his belt loops, Michael answered, "So now you're
interested?"

She touched the cross. Michael glanced above the rooftops, making it look a casual stray from her gaze.

"We will meet again, vampire," she said. "I promise you that. Until then, keep your head down and your teeth up."

Michael took two steps toward her—the flash of the cross burned his sight. Clenching his jaw tightly, he strained to move closer while he was forced to look away from the sacred.

The woman moved swiftly. She made the corner and disappeared.

Vampire. She did know.

Michael could not allow her to leave with the knowledge of what he was. He had to persuade her into thrall, make her forget.

Racing to the end of the alley, he barely avoided becoming roadkill. A chopper rumbled past him, the woman riding it not even glancing at him. On her back she wore two guns, holstered in crossed leather. Not the usual sight one expects to see in small town North Lake.

"Just my luck." Michael kicked the brick wall. "A slayer."

So why hadn't she done the deed?

For some reason, he must be worth more to her alive than as ash. But he wasn't willing to find out why. The longer a distance he put himself from an armed slayer, the better.

"Time to start that exile," he muttered, and strode the opposite way.

Chapter 3

Jane Rénan pulled her vintage red Mini Cooper up the drive before the Olson estate. Behind her by about twenty minutes traveled the delivery truck that transported her glass smith supplies.

She'd made a gentleman's agreement with the owner last winter during a stopover in Los Angeles, but hadn't been able to contact him last week to tell him she was now available to do the glasswork in his home. At the time, he'd said if the opportunity arose, she should begin the project. He'd even handed her a house key, proving his trust, and willingness to go ahead with the project.

It was imperative she be in town at this time, for the ritual must be completed during the full moon, and the one person who could provide her with a source for that ritual—Ravin Crosse—currently lived in Minneapolis. So Jane had shuffled her schedule to make things work.

A musician owned this house. Jane knew musicians. They were laid back, egotistic eccentrics, brash, outgoing savants, or quietly manic, desperate souls.

But most reassuring? They were even weirder than her own family. And even better? The famous ones had the cash to pay her well. And that cash afforded her the rambling, bohemian lifestyle she required to exist.

The pebbled drive crunched under her bare feet as she stepped out of the Mini.

Overgrown yew hedges in need of taming hugged the front of the two-story brick house. A honeysuckle vine climbed over the hedge tops, though it wasn't yet in bloom. A burst of brilliant gold forsythia hung over the front step, welcoming with a scratchy entrance.

Jane drew in a deep breath and centered herself, closing her eyes to focus.

The air was lighter here than in the city, the earth more verdant and alive. But to delve deeper, to draw in the very being of the atmosphere, she decided that this site lacked innate warmth. Nothing to make it feel like a home. It was private. And there was no magic here.

Perfect.

Walking the facade of the estate, the morning

breeze rippled the silk sari skirt Jane wore. Stitched with ornamental gold threading, it caught the afternoon sunlight in glints. A loose silk chemise skimmed softly across her breasts, and she pushed long faded strands of hair from her eyes as she scanned the upper floor.

"Should keep me busy," she remarked on the eight-foot high round-top windows at the front of the upper floor.

If those were the windows. Her notes stated the windows Mr. Olson had wanted done overlooked a garden.

Lifting her skirts knee high, she waded through the long, verdant grass—more a meadow than a yard—and around back. Drawn to a quick pace by the tempting scent of lilacs, Jane let out a gasp as she arrived in the backyard. Forgetting the windows, she glided toward the wild overgrown garden, her arms spread out to embrace the utter abandoned beauty.

Deep violet lilacs perfumed the air. A curious damselfly darted near her head. Leaves slithered against one another in a sinuous glide, and flower heads tilted toward Jane's feet. A sumac vine tendriled about her bare heel. She shook it off.

To avoid becoming entangled by overzealous flora she kept moving.

Plucking a frothy lilac panicle and twisting it under her nose, Jane could easily ignore the subtle movement all about her.

It is just you, Jane, her mother had once said. *There is magic within you. Don't let it scare you.*

She had never let it scare her. How could one be afraid of something they could not touch?

Glancing up to the windows, Jane winced as the noon sun reflected brightly at her. Half circle windows topped each slender eight-foot by three-foot picture window.

"Definitely the ones," she said. "I love the shape of them."

And she loved the circumstances.

This project provided the perfect working conditions. Peace and quiet, and freedom to create the designs she felt would complement the estate. And no owner to hang over her shoulder, wondering out loud how quickly it would be done.

But most important, privacy to prepare for the life-altering ritual that she must complete on the eve of the full moon.

Two hours later the truck driver had helped Jane unload sheets of colored glass and her supplies and tote them up to the second floor workroom.

Jane had opened up half the windows to let in some fresh air and expunge the staleness. She guessed this place must have been sitting closed up for well over a year.

Standing in bare feet before the windows and nursing a goblet of celebratory kir, she made a decision on the focus of her project.

"Art nouveau," she said. "A la Alphonse Mucha."

The nineteenth century artist's stylings would add the graceful elegance she sought for this room. In-

corporating curvy, flowing shapes—and a few surprises—into her designs would marry the house to
the outside gardens. Green, violet, red and brilliant
turquoise would give it a breathy lushness.

"It may even look a little rock 'n' roll by the time
I'm finished with it."

Glancing to the oversized sketchbook lying on the
makeshift worktable formed of a plywood plank and
two sawhorses, Jane decided she'd sketch out some
preliminary designs after a meal. Three bags of gro-
ceries waited downstairs on the cupboard, waiting to
be put away.

She intended to stay here while working on the
project. If the house was vacant, she often set up
camp. She never intruded too far into the owner's
property, occupying an extra room and using the
kitchen and bathroom. She'd leave the house as it
was when she'd arrived, if with a more splendid
view of the world.

After a quick supper of bread and cheese, Jane
explored farther and discovered a bedroom down
the hall from the workroom. Jane smoothed the soft
hemp sheets she'd brought along over the mattress,
anticipating a blissful sleep tonight. A dusty mirror
hung on the wall opposite the bathroom door. No
other furniture. Whitewashed walls granted an old-
fashioned country cottage coziness to the bare room.
She liked the cool emptiness; it fit her soul perfectly.

Padding about in the loose patterned pajamas
she'd changed into after a shower, she decided to

stroll outside and cut some lilacs for the bedroom. A little color would bring life to the room.

Using a utility knife from her equipment, Jane severed an armload of lilac branches, ignoring the soft moan that crept into the atmosphere with each slice through tender stem. She whispered blessings, and then went back inside.

Cradling her booty in one arm, she carried the heavy blooms inside to arrange in a shallow plastic tub she used for rinsing glass pieces. There were no dishes in the cupboards downstairs, so she'd make do.

It was still early, around six, so Jane finger-combed through her semi-dry hair and decided to wander about the house, take in the rest of the rooms.

The windows she'd spied upon arrival faced a hearth room clumped with massive pieces of furniture covered in stiff white canvas. That room, the workroom, a recording studio, and the one bedroom and bath made up the second floor. The first floor offered the same layout, yet was completely bare of furniture. There was also a basement, but there was no reason to check it out; it was likely empty as well.

The closest neighbors Jane could spot out the front windows lived over a mile away, beyond thick tracts of spindly birch and lush Northern pine and oak trees. This plot of land was truly a sanctuary. It wouldn't surprise her to see a grazing deer or two. With a smirk she decided the band could crank up their instruments to the highest volume and no one would hear.

Just across the hallway from the bedroom she had chosen, a recording studio was the only completely outfitted room in the house. Of course, a musician would concern himself with the tools of his trade.

Cautiously entering the studio, hands at her hips, she perused the equipment. None of it dusty. Must have recently been installed, or perhaps Mr. Olson sent a maid to freshen things up once in a while?

"It's a surprise that no one has tried to break in and steal this stuff." There was no security system, merely deadbolt locks on the outer doors.

The stacked black electronic equipment threatened Jane in an odd manner. She didn't like noise or the wildness of the world. Sure, she was an artist, but she preferred peace to an audience.

Sweeping her fingers over the mysterious sliding controls, she wondered at the use of each of them. There were dozens of small black plastic sliders. Each one must control a different part of the music, be it bass or treble or strings or whatever else it was musicians sang, played or yowled.

Smirking at the thought of a yowling musician, Jane snapped her finger over a black button.

The room yelled in protest. Rock music blasted at a decibel level to break glass.

Fingers shaking and her blood soaring to a buzz, Jane scrambled for the button she had just snapped. With another flick, silence befell the room.

"Bad Jane," she murmured, and then staggered out into the hallway.

Clutching her arms about her waist, she glared back at the evil room. The hairs on her arms stood upright. Her heartbeat threatened to leap right out of her throat.

That would teach her to play with other people's stuff.

"Guess I'll stay in my room and walk a wide arc around this one."

Another noise sounded suddenly, from somewhere at the end of the hallway. Footsteps tromping up a staircase. Someone was in the house?

"Who the hell—!"

The growl in that voice clued Jane she didn't want to stick around to wait for the bite.

Darting to the nearest retreat, she entered the bedroom. Slamming the door shut and locking it with the bolt and chain, she rushed across the room and scrambled for the utility knife she'd left beside the tub of lilacs.

A man's voice echoed from outside, growing stronger as he neared the bedroom door. "This is my place! You're trespassing! Open up!"

A firm kick on the opposite side set the door to shuddering.

Jane clutched the knife in her fist and crept toward the door. The thin bolt wouldn't keep the door closed forever. A scan of the room found nothing else that would serve as a good weapon, and the bed was too far to expend energy trying to push before the door.

She'd not intended to disturb anyone's privacy. This place was supposed to be unoccupied. Mr.

Olson should be out touring right now—he'd no plans to arrive until winter.

Which meant whoever stood outside the door was not welcome.

Chapter 4

Who the hell was in the house? He'd heard banging earlier, yet had dozed back to sleep. It hadn't been a peaceful rest, and the tunes had blasted any hope of shut-eye. Some drugged-up kid had likely broken in with intentions to trash the place. Well, he'd put a scare in the fool.

"Open up, you lousy piece," Michael snarled at the closed door. "This is private property."

"I was hired to work here!"

Michael stopped his foot from connecting with the door. A woman's voice?

"Who are you?" came from behind the door. "I was told this place was unoccupied. I've got a knife!"

He chuckled and pushed the hair back from his

face. So the greater forces didn't want him to make the leap to seclusion quite so quickly?

"Open up and we'll talk," he said, feeling his anger recede.

Drawing in a breath that sifted down to his gut quieted the turmoil within. And then he stretched his senses through the closed door to tap into the woman's heartbeats. He needed to feel her, to read her strength. To know who he was dealing with. Druggie or just an innocent woman?

"Not until you tell me who you are. Oh, what am I saying? I'm calling the police."

"Good luck with that," Michael called. "There are no phones hooked up in the place yet."

"I—I've got a cell."

Didn't sound too sure of that statement. Michael listened for the tiny beeps of a phone number being dialed. Nothing.

"This is my friend's house. Jesse Olson? He said I could use it for a few months." He slapped the door with the heel of his palm, knowing to beat on it would only frighten her further. Though he didn't sense fear. "I'm not a threat, I promise."

Well, not of the sort she might imagine. But she should be afraid. Very afraid.

Michael pressed his forehead to the door. He couldn't see her, but the smell of lilac pervaded any scent of fear he should be able to pick up.

She'd said she held a knife? That could make him bleed, but it wasn't going to slow him down.

Concentrating, he followed the heavy exhales of

her breath, tagging along with the inhales to enter her being. Once there, it was easy to tap into her heartbeat—furious and strong. Pulse racing, it teased him to the chase.

Trapped behind a door, with no exit, a pretty morsel waited to be devoured. Just a moment was all it required, and surrender—willing or not. So long as there was fear, and the adrenaline eddied in her blood. Like bloody champagne, he would drink her dry.

You're here to fight that craving, remember?

As if a whip to an open wound, a flicker of morality snapped Michael out of the blood reverie. He stepped back from the door, looking at it as if for the first time.

What was he doing? He had come here to beat the addiction.

"I—I think we've gotten off on the wrong foot. My name is Michael Lynsay. I'm sure you know me."

"Why should I know you?"

He could hear the rising confidence in her breaths. Calm crept in. Not so easy to surrender to his persuasion with confidence. Good. It would make resisting the temptation easier as well.

What had she said? She *didn't* know him?

"Don't tell me you've never heard of The Fallen? The hottest new band in the universe?"

"Mr. Olson is in your band?"

"You know Jesse? Right. You said you were hired?"

"To work on the stained glass Mr. Olson wants incorporated in the large back room. I…we had an agreement, but we'd never set an official date for the work to be done. I had some free time on my schedule. Mr. Olson hadn't mentioned there would be anyone staying here. And he did give me a key."

He did recall Jesse mentioning something about fixing the house up before moving in. Michael had thought it a waste of money for a home Jesse only planned to use a few weeks out of the year. And yet, the recording studio would lure the band then whenever they had free time. Or, in a pinch, it could serve as hideaway to a desperate vampire.

"You still holding the knife?"

"Yes."

Michael smiled. Pressing his hand to the door, he spread his fingers and closed his eyes. "You going to drop it?"

Silence.

And then— "I don't think so. I'm not stupid. A girl has got to be careful with strangers."

He fisted his fingers, prepared to bang the wood, to break down the barrier, but something made him pause. He wanted to get to the other side. Using force would frighten the spoils—not necessarily a bad thing—yet a nagging curiosity darted to the fore and claimed his persistent need.

Take this slowly. Enjoy the tease, and linger when finally the prize is won, yes?

Yes. Michael nodded. He could do slow. He didn't have to frighten them all. And until he knew what he was working with, he'd hold off on the fright fest.

"How do I know you are who you say you are?" she called.

Michael made a gracious sweep of his arm. "Open the door and see for yourself."

Such novelty. To control his need? And if she was pretty, well, nothing like indulging in some pre-exile debauchery.

"But I don't know your band. I rarely watch television or listen to popular music. I wouldn't know you from the cable guy."

"Insane," Michael hissed to himself. "Well, you're probably the only soul on this earth who hasn't heard of us. I've got a wallet and some ID downstairs. Hang on and I'll get it."

"I'm not going anywhere."

Chuckling, Michael went down the stairs and retrieved his wallet. If their positions had been reversed, he might insist that she do the same. Two years ago. Before he'd indulged in the adrenaline rush. Now? That door would have been kicked inside, no questions asked.

And yet he hadn't kicked it inside, even after tapping into her enticing heartbeat. That was surprising. Had the mere act of segregating himself from temptation already begun to work at the cravings eating away at him? He'd been here half a day. Was it to be so easy as this?

Striding back up to the second floor, he saw the bedroom door remained closed. He checked the knob. Locked.

Her lack of trust edged up a flicker of indignation.

And a sneer. Affront was the last thing he'd ever felt from the many fans who worshipped The Fallen. He wasn't quite sure how to deal with this new experience.

Tapping his foot, he counted to ten. It stopped the impulse to kick in the door.

"Here." He slipped his driver's license under the door. "I blinked when they took the picture. No such thing as do-overs at the DMV."

He didn't hear her pick up the small laminated card. Must be bending over it, inspecting.

"You were born in seventy-nine?" the woman asked.

"Yep, and it's my birthday soon." Yet he would forever remain ageless. "What about you?"

"Er…eighty-one."

"Weren't the eighties great?" Crossing his arms, he leaned against the doorframe. "Let it not be said the hair bands couldn't kick it with the best of them."

"I prefer the classics," echoed out the flat response.

The license slid back under the door. Michael retrieved it. And waited.

After what seemed like an hour, but was probably only a minute, the chain swung freely and the bolt shifted out from the lock.

Michael waited to allow her to shuffle away from the door, before twisting the old brass knob.

And in the next moment, when his instincts provoked him to leap and flash his fangs to ignite the fear, another part of him remained aloof, unwilling to react for the vision that stood before him.

Something indelible swirled out from the bedroom to caress Michael against the cheek. It entered his pores, invading on a mist of lilac, which shrouded any tint of blood scent. Her. Pale, lithe, flowing.

She stood as tall as he. All his life Michael had been athletic, yet awkwardly tall, which may be why he always noticed a woman's height first thing.

But the most amazing thing? That hair. Long breezy strands stained with copper here and there, but bleeding away to lighter, blond streaks elsewhere.

No makeup, not a hint of greasy lipstick or smelly black mascara. He liked that. And what a statement those pale parted lips made, though he knew she hadn't spoken.

From behind the warning of the utility knife, dark eyes glittered as if something secret and wonderful waited inside. Faery tales in her eyes.

Welcome to my grim tale, little girl.

"Nice." Michael stayed put. He could feel her anxiety push through the air and force an invisible hand against his chest. *Stay back.* No, it wasn't nervousness, but…command. She was not afraid. "I didn't get your name."

"Jane," she said, taking a bold step forward. "Jane Rénan. You got a cell phone?"

Fitting a palm to the doorframe over his head, Michael leaned inside the room. "I thought you did?"

"A necessary lie. But if you do, we can call Mr. Olson and clear up this whole mess *and* verify who you are."

"Come on, how many long-haired suede-pants-wearing freaks have you seen that didn't belong in a band? I'm legit, Jane. I promise."

"You had best hope so."

"You are a tough audience. I like that." He shrugged a palm up his arm, and the chain mail bracelet on his left wrist clinked against the thin silver band he hadn't removed in years. "I don't have a phone, it was part of the rules of my exile. No communication with the real world until I get my act together. I'm taking a break for a while. I'm…exhausted."

The word didn't sound right, no matter what spin he put to it. He'd leave that to the press, who had taken the rumor and rolled with it. By now, the evening entertainment news programs should be preaching his departure to the masses and spinning it to death, as well.

"Gotta rest and get my act together, you know?"

"And you're staying here to do that?"

He nodded. "Got in early this morning. I'm supposed to be hiding away. Do you know how hard that is for me?"

In but a blink of lash, she took him in, blond wavy hair to chain-wrapped boots. "I can guess that you must adore the spotlight."

He dropped his arms to hook his thumbs at the belt loops. *Look all you like.* "Am I that easy to read?"

She shrugged; the knife remained ready.

"You must have snuck in this afternoon. I heard banging, but thought I was having a bad dream until the music blasted. No one messes with the mix board."

"Sorry, I was curious. There was no car in the drive or the garage, and no sign the house was even occupied. Why were you sleeping during the day?"

"Rest, remember?"

Jane blew at a few strands of copper sneaking toward her eyelashes.

Kill me now, sweetly and savagely, Michael thought *Plunge forward and push the knife into me and spill that gorgeous hair over my face. Take me into your soul. I promise I won't bite.*

Maybe. Hell, what sort of idiot promise was that? Biting was the best part.

Damn, she was—otherworldly. That was the word. And standing there in thin purple pajamas, rimmed in fancy silver stitching, she looked like a doll fallen out from the toy box, wanting to venture out on her own—but not without a weapon.

She lowered the knife and shrugged a hand through her tousle of wild child locks. "I had intended to stay here while I worked on the windows."

"Ah." Not sure how to react to that one, Michael nodded, but perused the floor.

Another person inside his cozy little escape? Nothing wrong with that. And everything wrong with that. *People, you need a break from them, remember?* Right.

"It's cool," Michael rushed out before his conscience could protest. "The place is huge. We can both stay."

Even as she shook her head negatively he could

sense her surrender to the idea. Not your average woman, this girl. Jane. Simple name, but he suspected her soul was intricate and lush. And what he wouldn't give to push his fingers into her soul and crush it in a loose fist, allowing it to ooze down his arm and into his own twisted soul.

"I had hoped for privacy. Er, I have a...party planned in a few weeks," she said. "Wouldn't want to be in your way."

"I am a party kind of guy."

"Tea party?"

"Oh."

Tea? Maybe she wasn't quite the wild soul he suspected her to be. But those heartbeats...he could still feel them. As if he held them on his palm. And their perfect, calm rhythm was beginning to mess with his concentration.

Weird. Usually he couldn't tap a heartbeat unless he consciously tried.

Since when had he needed to focus so hard to hold a conversation with a woman? It wasn't as though he was an uncaged animal that would attack without warning. Michael Lynsay could work a crowd, appear normal before the press and at parties. He wasn't that far removed from humanity.

"I don't think this will work, Mr. Lynsay."

No kidding.

"It's just Michael. Mr. Lynsay is the name the record company uses when they're getting ready to lay down the law or hand me a list of all the wrong things we need to change on the album. Nice to meet you, Jane."

He held out a hand for her to shake. *Touch me. Feel the beat of your life. It's right there, in my hand.*

Knife wavering near her thigh, Jane studied his hand. Her pursed lips formed a pale bow. She would be so easy to take. One lunge, slide his hand up her back, coaxing her into his embrace, and she would be his. Forget the soul, he'd break his promise about not biting.

Hell. It would be complicated sharing the place, especially with temptation right under his nose. Temptation pounding in his temples, like blood rushing across his tongue and pouring down his throat in a sweet sticky fall of life.

Maybe that was what he needed? To be around it, yet know he couldn't touch it, because the consequences would prove harsh. He couldn't use this woman, and then walk away.

And why not? Who would miss her?

His best friend, who had hired her, and knew she would be here, for one. Michael would never hear the end of it if Jesse knew he'd bitten the woman he'd hired to do the windows.

Hadn't he slaked his thirst hours earlier? And he'd freaked himself because he'd almost killed the nameless blonde. Almost. He had seen her vein pulse.

He should not consider taking another victim so soon.

Not unless she was laced with adrenaline.

"Michael?"

In the periphery of his struggling thoughts,

Michael reacted to the vision before him as if he were pushing through a fog, and when through it, the room became clear and his senses twisted out of their pining desire for satisfaction.

And Michael smiled. Joy filled him. Quickly overwhelmed, he surrendered to the sudden emotion, the fruity, awkward lushness of happiness.

He looked down at his untouched hand, wondering, as Jane walked toward the far wall where a huge plastic tub of lilacs perched. She placed the knife on the marble counter. She hadn't touched him, and yet, he had felt her. Inside him. Like a pulse that commanded his own heartbeat. It had been... magical.

"I've no right to say whether or not you must go or stay." She crossed her arms and fixed him with a firm attitude. "But I'm not leaving, so I guess that means we must share. Which means, we'll need some rules."

Touch me again, he wanted to say. *Give me back that moment of lightness!*

Instead, Michael said, "I'll stay out of your hair."

It sounded good, but did he really believe he could keep his fingers from twining into that wild froth of sun-drained copper?

"I'll either be sleeping or in the recording studio. Deal?"

Her eyes shimmied from his face, over his arms and to his feet. She nodded.

He wondered if Jane was in the mood for a midnight snack.

Take it slow, the moral part that yet lived inside him suggested slyly. Draw it out. Seduce. Enjoy the lingering play. *It will be worth it.*

And if Jesse knew he had exiled the monster to live with a gorgeous beauty possessed of faery tale eyes? The man would have a cow.

Good thing there were no phones here.

Chapter 5

Michael stood in the kitchen, his back to the window that overlooked the gardens and the setting sun. He hadn't slept last night after meeting Jane. He didn't need to sleep any more than a few hours a day, though he often slept more simply because there wasn't a lot he could do in the daylight. Sure, he could go outside, even walk beneath the sun, but that lasted but a few minutes, before his eyes began to water and burn, and the feeling of such incredible loss of energy forced him back inside.

He wasn't about to explode into a million pieces like some of the more dramatic tales of vampires described. The burn ate much more slowly at his flesh, but it did burn, and he preferred to avoid the pain.

So. Here he stood. Not as alone as he'd intended. And nowhere near as calm as he felt his mission to beat the addiction should find him.

He was so aware, ultra alert to the other presence in the house. Even though she was on the second floor, at the other end of the building, and behind a closed door, Michael felt her heartbeat pulsing at the tips of his fingers.

He looked at them now. Tapped his middle finger to his thumb. Life. Intriguingly fresh and cloying in its presence. *Her life.*

This was not normal. He had no difficulty working a party or press event without once tapping into any of the myriad heartbeats that pulsed around him. He did not scent a potential victim's blood unless he focused, and centered onto that person. Reading the person for potential, gauging their interest in the man that stared at them, and their willingness to surrender to a force they couldn't explain, but innately felt. Called the persuasion, he used it sparingly, for more often than not, it wasn't difficult attracting a woman's attention.

So why could he swear he scented Jane now? Lilacs and powdery sweetness. All the way down here in the kitchen. It didn't seem possible. But it felt so real, he pressed his palm over his chest, as if to still the stir of her intrusion.

She, intruding into him? That's not the way it should go. He always intruded on them, teeth first.

"This is not going to work," he murmured. Sharing the house with a woman who tempted him even when out of his sight? "I'll have her on her back before morning, with her blood spilling down my throat. What's one more final hurrah before I go cold turkey, eh?"

It had to be this way. The habit was strong, sending out insistent urges to feed. Too bad there wasn't a twelve-step program for blood drinkers.

But until there was, Jane had better keep on her toes.

Jane was a little surprised Michael hadn't popped his head in to the workroom to check on her today. Not that she required checking up on, but it seemed odd, they two alone in this house, and to not talk? The door to the recording studio had been closed when she'd walked by earlier. He must be busy with tasks of his own.

Maybe it meant he was standing good on his word to stay out of her hair while she worked. Thoughtful of him. The last thing she needed was distraction. Even though—no, she shouldn't think it.

But she did.

She hadn't been able to remove his image from her brain as she slept a fitful night. Those eyes, so blue and delving, would not leave her thoughts.

A certain sensual awareness had oozed from the man like moonlight glimmering through a blue piece of glass as he'd stood in the doorway to the bedroom. Michael Lynsay absolutely glittered with appeal.

But she'd met appealing men before, and few of them had the same impact on her as this man did.

Sure, he was handsome—and, to judge from his cocky stance as he'd displayed himself for her to admire, he knew it. Tall men always attracted her, for they represented strength and longevity. Two very important requirements in any prospective man.

He'd stood in the doorway, legs spread and shoulders set back—commanding. Open to her, yet a little guarded. Or maybe it had been shyness? No, absolutely not.

And that sudden bright, friendly smile had really worked a number on her. Enough to keep her up thinking about him like some silly crushing fan girl.

"Oh, Jane, smarten up," she silently told herself.

Jane recognized the signs of an oncoming train wreck. She'd done artists, and a musician before. Love was too complicated. What if it didn't work out? A relationship with a man whose job description listed *spotlight* and *groupies* was not conducive to living the peaceful life she enjoyed. Nor should she even consider a relationship! This was a job, not a cozy singles' meet.

Had she done the right thing by agreeing to stay here with him? It wasn't as if he could go elsewhere—this was his friend's house.

But it wasn't as if she could leave, either. This location offered the privacy she required for the ritual.

In truth, she couldn't deny it felt good to have another presence in this big empty house. There were days she was too close to believing her father's claim that she'd become a hermit.

All she needed to do was figure out a way to ensure

Michael wasn't around on the night of the full moon. Nothing a concert at a local nightclub couldn't do to lure him. She'd have to check the local listings, so she could be prepared, and start dropping hints early.

The clunk of booted footsteps clued Jane that Michael walked down the hall toward the workroom. So he hadn't been in the studio, after all.

Jane pushed up her safety glasses—thick black plastic frames—and peered toward the open doorway, though the glasses distorted all things at a distance.

He'd stopped. Just outside the door? Or had he turned back?

Had she really heard footsteps?

Tilting her head and compressing her lips, Jane decided she must have invented the sound as an accompaniment to her busy thoughts. Although...

She waited. No, no one walked by the doorway.

Her skin prickled with an intuitive apprehension, so much so, that she looked at her arms to see the hairs had risen.

Hmm... She *was* sharing the house with a stranger. A man she knew nothing about. Just because he was famous didn't mean he couldn't also be a serial killer.

"Oh, brother." Rolling her eyes, and reaching for another piece of glass, Jane dismissed her idiot ideas.

Jane.

Pausing abruptly, the scratch of the steel cutting wheel over the smooth glass fumbled, and glass splinters serrated from the edge of the small piece. Jane pressed her fingers to her chest and drew in a breath. Had the wind whispered her name?

Twisting a look over her shoulder, she eyed the open window. Night had crept up on her without warning, and she could barely discern the outline of tall oak trees that bordered the property for the leaves joined and formed a frothy black mist that distorted her view of the waxing moon.

Shifting her weight from her left foot to her right set the hardwood floor to a groan. She'd been setting off that funky creak all day, but now, it sounded ominous.

Jaaa-ane.

Now that she heard.

Her name. No doubt about it. But not audibly spoken. Inside her head?

"*Mon Dieu,* the insanity in our family has finally touched me."

Unwilling to grant further merit to the eerie sensation, she set the glass cutter aside and marched over to the door. But her intent footsteps slowed as she gained the open doorway.

What did she hope to prove by checking around corners and speaking to the voices in her head? Only that she truly may be slipping into imagined insanity. It was not hereditary. She knew that for a fact.

"I've been working too long." With a sigh, she turned away from the door and took off the safety glasses.

A deep, commanding voice bellowed out of nowhere. Jane shrieked. A man appeared from outside the hallway.

Michael moved swiftly, taking her in his arms.

She suspected he realized he'd frightened her, and reached to console her. She tried to settle herself, but the weirdness of the moment tapped her last nerve and, as usual, she reacted with laughter.

Fright actually made her jump. Nice.

Michael leapt in for the attack. He grabbed Jane by the shoulders, tracking the scent of her fear, and swooped in toward her neck.

But too quickly, the vivid fear scent dissipated—to be replaced with giggles.

Caught up in the quest for a fix, Michael felt Jane's reaction as a slap to the monster's greed. He reeled back from her. Braced with hunger, and ready to feed, he had the sense to will his teeth back up into their sockets before she saw.

"Jane?"

"Oh!" Overtaken by laughter, she gestured at him with a loose hand, as she looked away and bent over double in mirth. "You frightened me!"

That had been the intention. But the result was far from satisfactory. Or, obviously, frightening.

"Do you often laugh at what scares you?" he asked. He had to know. For future attempts. And to sooth his bruised ego.

"No." She drew in a breath, then exhaled and fluttered her hand before her flushed face.

Copper hair spilled over her shoulders and called to his base desires. Wrap that hair around his fist and pull her to him for—

For what? A kiss? No, a long, deep taste.

What would she taste like? *Sin?* No, that was pushing it. A bit of proper unbound, this woman. Not completely removed from a self-imposed leash, he mused, but probably wouldn't protest too loudly should he sneak off the collar. So long as she didn't laugh.

"I was just feeling like someone was watching me, and then—well, you must have been walking by, and the sight of you scared me."

"I see."

He reached to smooth away a strand of hair that had gotten caught on her eyelashes. But in actuality, Michael wanted to feel that fiery red cheek before the blush completely dissipated. The color faded immediately, and so he drew back his fingers just before they contacted her pale skin.

"I have been known to raise a scream or two from women, but never laughter at the sight of me."

"I'm so sorry." Hands propped upon her hips, Jane settled herself.

Michael fixed his gaze to the sensuous slide of thin silk across her full breasts, tight there, where her nipples poked out temptingly. He diverted his eyes, slowly, down the slender curve of her waist, and to just above her hips where the skirt clung. Could he span that narrow waist with both hands? Most definitely.

And that hair! It had a mind of its own, probably even its own personality, and right now the copper and blonde strands were laughing at Michael.

"Did you…" She sucked in another deep breath, and finally spoke with calm. "Did you say my name?"

"No," he lied. He hadn't exactly spoken it aloud. But never before had the persuasion served him such ridiculous results.

"Huh. Thought I heard my name."

"And that's why you were so fearful?"

"I wasn't afraid."

Oh, yes she had been. He'd scented her fear, or rather, a heightened awareness that had tread the edge of fear. It had been delicious. And his leap into the room should have released the adrenaline throughout her system, flooding her veins with a heady treat for him.

"Are you hungry?" she suddenly wondered. "I'm ready to call it a night. Haven't eaten all day. I was thinking of taking supper out back so I could explore the garden in the twilight."

"Hungry." He traced his tongue along his upper teeth, his lips closed. "I was, but my appetite has suddenly gone. But I will join you outside. Twilight is my favorite time to be with a beautiful woman. The light tends to fall just so upon all that she can be."

Her eyes brightened. The rejection Michael had received from her reactionary laughter subsided.

So she wasn't afraid of a good scare? Next time, he'd have to be subtler.

"I'll meet you outside," she said.

Chapter 6

Jane had gathered some fresh fruit in a bowl and mixed two goblets of kir—crème de cassis poured into champagne and strolled out to sit in the grass before the garden.

Michael showed up moments later. Sunglasses sat upon his head, though it was indeed twilight. The fact that he'd made a point of bringing the glasses along was curious.

He settled into the overgrown grass beside her and leaned over her shoulder to inspect the booty. "I love cherries."

"Have at them." She pushed the glass bowl of fruit toward him. "I don't know why I bought them, because they're not my favorite. Guess they looked too good to resist."

He picked around a piece of cut watermelon and claimed a ripe black cherry and popped it in his mouth. "You have difficulty resisting things, Jane."

She smirked at his teasing question. And yet, it had been more rhetorical. "Not men, Michael, just food."

"Harsh."

She turned to offer him a smile, but the sight of cherry juice drooling across Michael's lower lip startled her. A thin stream of crimson glistened upon his lip.

Jane gasped. Instinctively she reached for the wound, but—*no, it's not a wound*. What strange memories the sight dredged up. Not even strange, mostly…familiar.

She looked away. Had her heart fluttered a little faster? Silly woman, he was eating cherries with red juice. What did she expect?

But she couldn't prevent herself from looking back. Michael chewed and then spat the entire fruit over his shoulder into the grass. "You don't eat the whole thing?"

His tongue slipped out and dashed along his lips, the action wicked and more than a little tempting.

"I like the taste of them, but I never swallow. The flesh is…I don't know, not right going down." He set the bowl in his lap and counted the small red fruits. "Eleven," he announced.

"I see." She turned away, admonishing inwardly at her quickened heartbeats.

If she so much as thought about the image of a

man with a deep red stain on his lips, she'd have to laugh. Michael was certainly not—

He popped another cherry into his mouth. Juice splashed his lower lip.

Oh, please, now he's just doing it to get a rise out of me.

Yet her unease did not dissipate, and so in order to avoid it, Jane forced herself to focus on other things.

Finishing off the goblet of kir, she then stood and approached the massive stone fountain she had spied from the upper floor. The head of a cherub peeked above a tight twist of emerald vine as if gasping out one last breath before being completely tugged under. The entire fountain was overgrown with weeds and climbing sumac that wielded three-pointed leaves of green shiny leather. The sumac tickled at her ankles, and forced her to step constantly in a sideways march about the fountain.

Michael followed her to the garden's edge, hands hooked at his hips, legs spread in an aggressive stance. He wore soft brown suede pants and a black T-shirt. Everything about him looked touchable. Accessible.

Are you available for a wicked liaison?

Michael smiled a daring grin, as if he sensed her thoughts.

Avoiding the man's searching blue gaze, Jane grabbed a bunch of dried vines and leaves and tugged them from the cherub's bow and quiver of arrows. The desiccated foliage gave easily, and did not cry out. She dropped it on the ground, right on top of the creeping sumac. That gave it pause. Good.

"Would you mind?" she said. "Give the bowl a shove to get it back on center."

Michael stared at the heavy stone piece, looking as if he couldn't decide where to touch it.

"Don't tell me." Jane blew rogue strands of hair from her eyelashes. She kicked at a nuisance vine creeping up the back of her leg. "The rock star isn't up for manual labor?"

"I have people who do this kind of stuff for me."

That impressed her not at all.

"And here I thought you'd earned those biceps muscles. What are they, part of the costume? Earned by catching women's panties?"

Michael chuckled, tilting his head back in a grand gesture. "Oh, lady, if you only knew." The gaze he fixed on her spoke a malevolent charm. Deadly, and yet, enticing.

"Well." She fisted her hands at her hips and kicked down the vine climbing her ankle. "I'm sure I don't want to know."

"Panties *and* bras," he corrected. "You wouldn't believe the collection we had on the bus."

"I'm sure I wouldn't. But I guess you appreciate that aspect of the job."

"Wouldn't you? If some man tossed his boxers your way—"

Jane put up a palm to stop him. "Please, Michael. Keep your boxers on."

"I don't wear boxers."

A lift of her brow, and her eyes strayed to his

crotch. One thing about musicians, they liked to wear their pants tight.

Michael met her distracted gaze with a daring grin. His lip curled up on the right side—cherry-stained temptation—and it only enticed her all the more.

Watch it, Jane. You're not supposed to let them see you peek.

She stroked the smooth edge of the stone bowl. "Despite what men tend to believe, we women prefer a man to keep his panties on."

"Boxers."

"Whatever." Now she was just being silly. Was it so easy for her to fall for a sexy smile and a dangerous glance? "What men need to understand is that we women are not visual like you." Well. Okay, maybe a little. "We prefer the seduction and romance of foreplay to a silly display."

"I'll grant you that, though I wouldn't call it a silly display."

"I'd call slinging one's underwear through the air silly."

"To each his own. But I do know a little about women."

"Don't you mean groupies?"

He continued, "*Women* need seduction. The sweet nothings, the long, drawn-out foreplay. Roses and chocolates and all that romantic fluff. Fair enough. It serves a purpose. But we guys? We are all about the tangible." He rubbed his thumb and forefinger together. "Let us see it, smell it, touch it and taste it. Oh, man, do I love to taste it."

Jane quirked a brow at his confession. Didn't sound half bad, she decided. The man could taste her any time. Truly. She just wondered how long it would be before he attempted it. Because she wouldn't push him away. Michael Lynsay was not the sort of man any sane woman would push out of her bed. And she was sane, and on the verge of becoming a hermit.

She needed a man. In her bed. To remind her that she had not completely fallen asleep to life.

Pacing around the fountain, she listened to his boots slash through the long grasses.

"You don't wear panties or a bra," he commented in that same tone that tingled across her scalp and further heightened her awareness of his closeness. "I can tell. Those strappy shirts you wear are thin as tissue paper and I know there's nothing underneath except skin and tits."

Jane snapped upright and, when she wanted to blast out how rude his comment was, she stilled her retort.

Michael didn't stand on the other side of the fountain. She bent to see if he'd squatted on the ground on the other side of the wide fountain base. Not there.

The trace of wind through her hair, a little rougher than it should be, made her spin about to find herself less than a step away from the leering singer. Yes, he leered. Nothing whatsoever enticing about that triumphant grin.

"I—I," she fumbled for a reply, "didn't see you move."

"Just checking for panty lines," he offered coolly. "None."

He gave a shove with his hip against the fountain bowl and the heavy stone basin slid into place. Now that was a triumphant, if a little arrogant, grin.

"You don't have people to do that," she protested.

"Just playing with you. I like to tease. Your reaction tells me a lot about you."

"Really?"

"You're guarded, but sometimes you can be more open. If you think it'll get you what you want."

"You some kind of shrink?"

"Ha! No, just an interested observer of the common woman."

Common. So like normal. Normal was all Jane had ever strived for. She'd come so close, had resigned herself to the mundane. Order, and keeping certain kinds of influence at a distance had always served her need for control.

And now this man had charged into her well-ordered world, spouting his personal doctrine of panties, music and cherry juice.

Still, the image of the juice streaming over his lip disturbed her. It shouldn't, but it did.

"I think you are the furthest thing from common," she blurted out.

"I'll buy that. I do get paid to be a showman. Seduce the fans to sing the music. Buy the music. Fill the stadium. Smile for the cameras, Mr. Lynsay, show us the fallen angel's sad smile."

"And you're quite self-occupied."

"Interesting deduction." Michael leaned over the stone bowl. "And what about you? You are more uptight than your free-as-the-breeze earth mother appearance lets on."

"My—" Free as the breeze? Earth mother? Is that how he had summed her up? Jane wasn't sure how to take that assessment. She wasn't free as— But she should be. Her lusting soul certainly craved the adventure of another. "Don't you have some music to blast?"

"You sick of talking to me? You were the one to invite me out here."

Rain splatted on Jane's nose. Another drop landed Michael's cheek. Nothing steady, just a fine, intermittent mist.

He tilted his head, studying her, but made no move to step closer.

Jane felt the curve of the fountain against the backs of her calves. The edges of sumac leaves tickled the tops of her feet.

"I...er..." She slipped to the right and bent to feel under the fountain bowl. Grasping the vine tangled about her left ankle, she ripped, choking it from its roots. That'd teach it. "There must be a switch or something along the base. Don't you think?"

"Why are you frightened of me, Jane? I won't hurt you. Do I come off as some kind of monster to you?"

Her fingers played over a small button. Pressing it, Jane heard water begin to gurgle within the stone foundation of the piece.

She stood and brushed back her hair. Her arms were moist with mist, and running her palms over the front of her chemise reminded her of what Michael had correctly deduced about her lack of undergarments. She didn't need a bra. Besides, she hated feeling confined.

"You're not a monster," she said. "And you're right, I don't know you, so even if you were…"

"Which I am not."

"Sure. But grant me this I have volunteered to stay with a stranger, and will remain cautious until we do—" *Get to know each other,* got stuck at the back of her throat. Sounded too committed. But the need for connection was so strong. This man attracted so easily. Common? Was that how he labeled all his groupies? "Oh, here it comes!"

Water splashed out of the cherub's pursed mouth and—well, it was more a drool down the chin and fat belly that then routed to a few trickles across the toes and into the bowl.

"Give it a few minutes," Michael said. "The water pressure will increase." He stepped back, and Jane took a step at the same time.

Turning swiftly, Michael caught Jane from falling by grasping her shoulders. Supporting herself by gripping his shirt front, she chuckled—fear reaction.

And he leaned in to kiss her.

The fine translucent jewels of rain coating Michael's hair slid down Jane's cheek. He smelled of rain and grass and black cherries. He tasted wild. And sinful. Ending the kiss, he nudged into her hair and snuck kisses along her neck.

His hungry groan matched her own wanting

murmurs. Jane clung to his shirt, unwilling to release him. Teeth grazed the underside of her jaw, seemingly gentle strokes promised danger when he passed over the thick vein.

Whatever he was to the world, his fans and the groupies, he was certainly not common. His heart pounded against hers, the bass beat of a frenzied Indian powwow.

He felt…familiar. A wicked disease shivered up Jane's arms. Was it the anxiety of a new kiss? Or the longing familiarity of so common an act?

Not common, this man. Wicked and unique.

But he belonged to the world. To all those many worshippers. Why did she feel as if she were stealing him away from all of them? And what was wrong with that?

A glance of skin on skin traced her back, his fingers explored her spine, heightening her senses. She could smell his being, salty and strong, and taste his want, even feel his curiosity. Slither and glide, two fingers skated up her spine, beneath her silk shirt. Jane moaned. The touch, it—

What was that odd feeling?

The shimmer?

Michael's eyes snapped open and his clear blue eyes focused on hers. He shifted his body to fit tight to her hips and chest and legs, pressing fingers against the small of her back as if he wanted to push her right through him. A silent challenge was issued.

Compelled by primal instinct and the desire for

contact with a potent male, Jane moved into him. Sliding her knee between his parted legs, she crushed her chest against his. Her nipples hardened against his tight pecs. A shiver engulfed her body.

Yes, it was the shudder of kissing a stranger, not the shimmer. That was ridiculous to even consider.

"I could take you right here," he groaned.

"You don't even know me."

"Are you afraid of a stranger's desire? That I want you?"

She closed her eyes and let her head fall back. Her hair dusted Michael's elbows. He held her there, so covetously. She could feel his erection against her thigh, powerful and strong, wanting, and yet, not so demanding as to make her feel threatened.

Afraid? Never.

But cautious? Always.

"I bet you ask all the girls that before you make love to them, then walk away, never again to see them."

"Judgmental, aren't you? What makes you think I have had so many girls, and then walk away?"

"Isn't that what rock stars do?"

"Oh, Jane, you have no idea what I am. Rock star is just the costume I wear."

His roaming kisses found her mouth, and he clasped the back of her head, drawing her deeper into the intimate play. *Mine,* the move said. *Will you surrender?*

The answer came unbidden. Jane allowed her body to melt into his every hardness and angle. Her fingers stroked the flexing muscles on his arms. His every movement changed the sinew and flesh beneath her caress, tightening it, stretching it. Whatever lay beneath the costume, she wanted a peek.

She stepped a bare foot onto his boot. A moan escaped. Want cried out. Yes, she wanted, groupies be damned. Begone the other sensation currently tracing the back of her neck and tingling across her scalp. A warning? No, the danger she had seen in him earlier, when he'd scared her in the workroom, wasn't there now.

"Then let me see beneath the costume," she said, clinging to his T-shirt, wanting to tear it from his hard body, but using it more to merely hold on to a last vestige of common sense. "Right here."

Forget common sense. She had been a good girl for far too long. She worked hard, supported herself, and always—well, usually—did what was expected of her. Didn't she deserve a dance with this dangerous bit of sexy?

"Ah!" Michael suddenly pushed away from her, separating their bodies with a rush of cool, misted air.

Stretching back his shoulders and spreading out his arms, he tilted his head back, and like a mighty warrior, cried out to the star-speckled sky.

Unsure how to react, Jane stumbled backward, but caught herself against the fountain.

Without looking at her, Michael twisted at the hip and strode toward the house. "Sorry! I…"

The insurgence of sensation—at her lips, in her breasts, pulsing in her groin—receded as quickly as it had begun. Jane stood there, empty, and open, breathing heavily.

A shiver scurried through her body, and she clutched her arms, hugging herself. She had felt him. Like a whisper in her blood. An invitation to dance in his exotic world.

She touched her mouth, hot and plumped from the ravaging. "Yes, ravaged," she whispered.

Instinctually, she knew it was the man's mind she had labeled, and not their embrace.

Chapter 7

What novelty. Michael Lynsay had refused to follow through with a seduction.

Why? Because after that first kiss, well then, the next kiss, and the next just wouldn't be as exciting. Or that's what Michael told himself as he cruised toward town in Jane's Mini Cooper.

Truth was, if he had wanted to continue kissing her, the monster would have barged in, begging him to bite. And after the bite, the kiss didn't matter any more. Persuasion would be called upon. Jane would swoon into his bite, and later, she would come to without memory of the extraction.

That he'd been able to push away from Jane and resist going further gave him minimal hope. He *could* control his urges.

What he couldn't do was this *sharing the space* bit. Which is why he pressed the accelerator to the floor.

"Lousy seventy miles per hour on this thing," he muttered. "Piece of junk."

In response, the Mini started to shake as it rumbled over the gravel road. Michael let up on the gas and the car settled to a smooth fifty miles per hour.

He hadn't asked to borrow Jane's car, but he intended to gas it up in thanks. It had been all he could do to get out of the house and away from the woman. And her heartbeats.

He flexed his hand, sensing she had not followed him into his pulse. This felt too fast. Yes, even for him, a man who could take a nameless woman behind an alleyway after a concert, this was fast.

But only because this time it felt like it should be more than a mere fix. Something about Jane compelled him, made him want to slowly peel away her layers to discover the riches inside. It was more than a blood craving.

Why did he feel her inside him?

This was new to him, so he wasn't sure how to define it. But he did want more. More Jane. More kisses. And sure, sex, as well. But not until he'd collected himself.

His stomach lurched painfully. The constant feeding he'd conditioned his body to withstand would never allow him to forget when it was time for sustenance. Hell, not even sustenance, it was the need for adrenaline, plain and simple.

Why did sex—not even sex, but simple kisses

and foreplay—always summon the urge to drink blood?

It had been decades since he'd been able to make love to a woman without then drinking from her. When wrapped within the blood hunger, his lust began to frenzy. He needed satisfaction. But mere orgasm no longer did it for him. The monster demanded its fill.

The monster wrapped chains about the man who wanted to kiss her—*just taste Jane's sweetness*—and instead made him pay with blood.

A tiny prick at his temple promised to become a fierce screw drilling into his brain should he not pay attention to his body's demands.

"Don't worry, you bastard," he muttered. "I'm looking."

"Frickin' flames." Ravin Crosse stabbed the point of her dagger onto the fluttering white flyer that had been stapled to the wall in the hallway leading to the restroom.

She glanced out to the main floor of the Denny's restaurant. Patrons were eating, conversing, paying her no mind.

Tugging the flyer loose, she stuffed it in a pocket and went out the side door. Her chopper was parked in the lot across the street, right next to the Dumpster, where no one ever parked.

Straddling the leather seat, she then drew out the flyer and unfolded the crumpled white paper. The five men who formed the group The Fallen stared at her. They were playing a concert in two nights at the Decadance, a nightclub located just out of North Lake.

The man in the center of the photo, the tall one with the long blond hair and killer smile, taunted the camera with a gimmee gesture of his fingers. Ravin recognized him immediately.

"Not good," she said to herself. It was the vampire she had pinned as a source.

"Curse them all! A public figure would certainly be missed if he suddenly ceased to exist."

Tearing up the flyer, she then balled it up and tossed it into the Dumpster. "Jane is not going to like this."

"Looks like a schedule of tour dates from last year," Sylvan Banks commented. He handed the iPod to his mistress. "You can store a lot of info on these little things. Yes, like that. You swing your forefinger around the white dial. Do you see that list of files? You can select one by pressing the center button. Do you want me to do it?"

"I'm not stupid." The woman drew her shoulders away from the irritating man. Still barely a teenager, he tried her every last bit of patience with his obnoxious need to treat her like an invalid who could not even understand the simplest of tasks.

She leaned over the small white music player to study the device, but her focus strayed.

She was exhausted. Tired, and so ready to release the tattered shroud from her body and step back into life. It had been over a year, and still the healing moved at a snail's pace. She could barely see a change in the ruddy lumps and puckers that had invaded her flesh.

Devastated by the ugliness of her condition, she rarely went out at night, and relied on lackeys like this boy to bring her sustenance.

This was not like her. Once she had been strong, bold and beautiful. So beautiful, they always cried, just before climax. That she had not died a year ago only proved she was meant to walk this earth. But not like this. She missed her lovers. She craved the affection, the blind worship and sexual play.

Until her confidence returned, she would not have any of it. And that was only possible with the help of one very important man.

She scanned the list of files on the music player Sylvan had found in the graveyard. Music. Videos. Podcast? Whatever that was. Tour schedule. Songs. Unfinished.

So much inside this little bit of plastic. She did not cease to marvel at technology. And when she thought she'd learned all she could about gadgets and gizmos, another new one emerged to be discovered and marveled over.

"You're sure it belongs to him?"

"Picked it up from the top of his mother's grave. It's his."

"This piece of his life does me little good, especially, as you've explained, with the ear pieces missing. Is there an address for Mr. Lynsay in there? Or rather, look up all his band mates, and check for

Minnesota addresses. Is there any way we can get a message to him via that thing?"

"You mean like a video? Sure, that's possible. I just need to download the software and I've got some video equipment. What sort of message?"

"You worry about the electronics, I'll contend with the words. Got it?"

"Yes, Isa—er, mistress."

Idiot. She'd found Sylvan an agreeable enough lackey when she'd first tracked him down through the music magazine. The reporter had written an article about The Fallen. While no expert on the group, he did live in Minnesota, which made tracking them easier.

Soon, very soon.

And then?

Back to life.

She returned his wink from across the dance floor. The club was virtually dark, save the frenetic strobe that glimpsed bits of laughter, gyrating hips, swaying arms and bouncing breasts.

Michael strode toward the back door, knowing she would follow. He high-fived a young man who pointed in recognition at him, and then shoved open the back door. It had stormed briefly this afternoon, and now the heat had stirred the atmosphere into murk. Fog coated the air.

"Is it really you?" giggled up behind him. His catch for the evening. "The fallen angel?"

Pretty damn close.

"Shh." Michael stretched back his hand and she clasped it. "No talking, sweetie."

"But I'm going to need an autograph. Please? Oh, pretty please?"

"How can I say no to a pretty please like that? This way."

He spied a hedge that bordered the back of a Chinese restaurant. The smell of orange chicken and spicy shrimp called to him. The love for aromas never left, though to eat would make him physically ill.

"Come here." He tugged the woman to his side, and insinuated them behind a delivery truck with a cold engine.

The restaurant was still open. Clanks of dishes and shouts echoed out through the back screen door. They'd have to be quiet. Which meant, as soon as he flashed his fangs, he'd have to slap a hand over her mouth.

"Ready for this?" He eased her hand over his crotch to throw her off the plan.

"I'm so excited. A real rock star! I saw you on MTV!"

"Yeah, baby. Whatever."

He didn't bother to kiss her. Kisses, while intimate, didn't appeal when the women slathered thick goop all over their lips. She stroked him hurriedly.

"Hey, baby, take a look at these, will you?"

He tilted his head down and stretched open his mouth. An appropriate evil growl felt right.

As predicted, her scream was easily silenced with

a clamp of his wide hand over her mouth. Michael worked quickly to satisfy the monster.

Startled awake by the garage door opening and closing, Jane sat up and swung her feet out of bed. Shrugging a hand through her tousled hair, she yawned and stretched. It was still dark out; the moon scythed high in the sky.

A car door slammed. Must be Michael. He'd taken her car without asking, but she hadn't minded. Though she did mind the fact that he'd seemed to be fleeing her after almost convincing her to have sex with him in the garden.

What had she said to turn him off so completely?

Heck, she had been *willing*. Which didn't speak well for her powers of attraction. Had she forgotten how to turn a man on?

It wasn't as if she hadn't experience. How long had it been since she'd slept with a man? To think about it was more depressing than she was willing to admit.

Well, she was up. Might as well go say hello, see if he was in the mood to talk.

Quickly descending to the main level, she spied Michael as he came toward her down the hallway. He looked a marvelous splendor. Blond hair flowing behind him with his quick pace, his arms he held slightly arced out at his sides.

"Michael." Jane realized she clung to the chair rail nailed hip-level on the wall, and released her tight clutch. "Just getting home?"

Though the hall was dark, his eyes glittered and his teeth flashed as he answered, "Yep."

He smelled like smoke and alcohol, and something innate. Jane could not name the familiar scent, yet it disturbed her.

"I don't mind you taking the car," she offered.

"I gassed it up."

"Thanks."

He paused at the end of the hallway, facing the stairs that led to the basement where he must have his own room—though Jane had respectfully kept away from snooping. Twisting his neck as if to fight out a kink, he then turned to her.

Sighing through his nose, now that he had stopped moving he seemed to fill the entire hall, his presence soaring beyond the physical body and becoming a part of the very air.

Jane drew in a breath. Smoke. "You've been to a club?"

"Yes." He stalked closer.

She realized she wore nothing but thin silk pajamas. And yet, approached by the man, she did something entirely unexpected. Instead of crossing her arms over her chest, she put back her shoulders, which lifted her breasts. The hallway light, located thirty feet away, cast a soft glow over them.

She felt…frisky. And wanting. Things inside of her had gone missing. Or rather, she couldn't name the source of emptiness; it could be inner, or maybe it was external. All that surrounded her demanded focus, and yet, something was missing. Nothing tangible though—she felt that. Something inside awaited release. *Awakening.*

Could she possibly seduce him this time?

As Michael stopped before her, she couldn't read his shadowed eyes.

"There's a place called the Decadance close by," he said. Pressing the heel of his palm to the wall over her shoulder he leaned over her. Instantly arriving at the aroused state she'd achieved with the garden kiss, Jane breathed shallowly. "The band is playing there in a few days, sort of a homecoming concert. I'd like you to come."

Oh, she could come. In more ways than one. Just one touch from him and Jane felt pretty sure her body would leap into the adventure of sex with a stranger.

She lingered on the closeness of him, his presence. *His wicked danger.* She'd felt it before. It was a solid intuition. What could possibly be dangerous about a rock star? (Besides everything?)

His eyes dragged across her face, not so soft as she wanted the seduction to be, but it was his manner. Masculine, viral, imposing his presence upon her with an intimate cleverness. "You'd pretty up the venue."

Pretty up?

Come back down, Jane. Step out of the fantasy and back into the real world.

"Is that how you choose your dates? For their aesthetic value?" Her sexual desire deflated. "I suppose it is a requirement that you be seen with a certain type on your arm."

"You're that type."

He reached to stroke her mouth, but Jane jerked away and slid a few paces along the wall. Now she did cross her arms over her breasts, hiding her erect nipples. How quickly her body jumped into the sexual play, while her brain wanted to think things through.

"I'm no such type. I'm not like your...women."

Michael chuckled and leaned against the wall next to her. He faced the opposite wall, shoulder close to hers, but no connection. His hips, thrust out, screamed for her to take notice, to see what a man he was. All muscle and brawn and superstar confidence.

"And how do you know what my type is, Jane? I'll have you know I never invite women to the show. I don't do dates. Rarely do I even do girlfriends."

"Just quickies with groupies, then?"

He turned so quickly, Jane flinched, upon viewing his face.

Just as quickly, he retreated and spread his fingers to scruff through his hair. But she had seen. A violent reaction to her tease. She hadn't meant to rile him, but that his ire could be so easily stirred bothered her.

She checked her desires. Probably not so safe to fall into the sex with a stranger fantasy, as she'd previously thought.

"I should get back to bed," she said. "I've been working long days."

"I'm sorry," he offered. "Jane. I know I scared you. I've just...been tense lately."

"Hardly the way to begin a relaxing vacation."

"No kidding. Honestly, I don't think I know how to relax. How to come down from the stage, slip off the costume and just be me."

Jane was aware of his gaze tripping over her face and down her neck. He paused on her breasts, still concealed by her crossed arms. He made no move to disguise his interest, in fact, he wanted her to notice it, she felt sure.

"I want to kiss you again," he said. "I promise I won't leave like I did in the garden. It was just a surprise to me."

"That I was so easy? I don't normally kiss strangers."

"I'm not a stranger, Jane." He pressed an arm high along the wall and leaned his forehead against the crook of his elbow. "Promise I won't scare you anymore. Deal?"

She shrugged. Even tainted with smoke, he smelled…like something she wanted to know. "And how to seal such a deal?"

Now he traced her mouth. She didn't see the move, and yet once he touched her, she did not flinch.

"I can't promise to be a gentleman," he said, his voice husky with recognizable want. "That's not my style. I see something, I take it."

"I remember. You like to see it, touch it—"

"Taste it. There's something about you, Jane, that won't leave me. It's like you're inside of me, your perfume, it calls to me."

"I don't wear perfume."

"I know." He breathed on her chin. Jane locked her knees, so she wouldn't collapse and fall into his arms. "It's the perfume of you, sweet and alluring. It's all over me. Makes me want to be right next to you. Can you feel it?"

She clasped his hand, but held his fingers on her lips. "I've always been ultra sensitive to people. Maybe you're mirroring my sensitivity?"

"Could be. Or maybe I just want you."

Michael leaned in to Jane's wild copper hair and whispered against her ear. "Have you ever felt another person's heartbeats inside your own veins?"

Her soft exhalation floated across his mouth. Each breath lifted her breasts against his chest. Her nipples aroused his libido. *Eat in her surrender.* She was his.

He wasn't willing to so abruptly halt things this time around, but he had to play it cautiously. No more surprises.

He'd sated his thirst earlier in town. Now he had the freedom to play.

"Can you feel my heartbeats?" she whispered.

"Of course. But they're very calm. Jane, what does it take to arouse you?"

She tensed at the slide of his hand along her neck. The vein was not so prominent; her flesh expertly hid her treats. Further exploring, he dipped a finger into the clavicle at the base of her neck and traced slowly. Delicate bones there beneath the skin. The rise of her breath pushed up the tops of her breasts. Still, her heartbeats were solid, a bit faster, but nowhere near fear. Which was fine. He wasn't looking for that kind of fix.

"A kiss," she prompted. "You'd wanted but a kiss?"

"Only if you want it."

He bent to touch with his tongue the shallow indentation at the base of her neck. Her skin heated at his touch, he could actually feel the rise in her temperature.

"Do you want it?"

"Yes," she said on a sigh.

This deliciously common mortal had fallen to his seduction.

What wasn't common was his gentle investigation of her curves and angles. When was the last time he'd allowed himself the leisure to stroke a single finger along a woman's skin? To listen to what she sounded like when her breath tread the line between curiosity and abandon.

And if this was all it required for him to learn to control the inner monster, then bring on the practice. Lots and lots of slow perusal and kisses.

He folded his fingers along the edge of the silk pajama top. Silver threading stitched through the superfine fabric in a fancy arabesque. It felt sharp and he wondered if it bothered her tender skin.

"The kiss?" she reminded.

"You're very impatient, Jane. Besides, I didn't specify where." Leaning in, he blew a breath upon the gentle plunge that centered between her breasts. "I'm trying to locate a good spot."

While intent on tracing a finger along the silver threading, moving excruciatingly slowly along the rise of her breast, he was aware she pressed her fingers to the wall near her hips. Granting him free rein. Opening herself to whatever adventures his journey took them on.

And so he didn't even consider the persuasion, which was the lulled, calming state he could easily entice a potential victim toward with but a few careful thoughts. No, he didn't want to interfere with Jane's mental state. He wanted to see exactly how far he could take this before she protested.

And then? Well, then he'd deal with the monster should it stomp its foot in protest.

"Tell me where you want it," he said. "Where shall I kiss you, Jane? On the mouth? Here, at the base of your neck?"

He blew across the rise of her breasts. He had not yet brushed the hard nipple that pleaded for attention. The denial of that pleasure increased his yearning measurably. "Or here, above your heartbeat?"

He didn't know when she'd removed her tense fingers from the wall, but the touch of her nails, gliding up the back of his scalp and burying themselves in his hair made him aware that he was completely aroused, and very ready. His erection tightened inside his pants. He needed to expend the sexual energy that had been drawn to the surface earlier tonight.

And with his arousal, came the hunger—which didn't surprise him in the least.

His canine teeth tingled, signaling the craving that accompanied the act of foreplay. He didn't want that to happen. So he concentrated on keeping back the evidence that would surely make her scream— and fulfill his twisted addiction—if only as experimenting with his own self control.

"Right there, where you breathed," she said in a breathy rush. Her fingers pressed against his skull, imploring him to move in close, and so he did.

His tongue landed on the unreal heat of her skin. A burn, a sweet fiery brand, marked him indelibly. Michael moaned against her breast and pressed his lips above the silk. She arched back her shoulder, lifting herself against his lips, and he opened his mouth in a reactionary bite, but at the last moment, he covered his teeth with his lips to soften the connection.

"And where else?" he prompted, eyeing his next desired location. "Show me."

Her hand slipped down from his head and glided across his fingers. Following her direction, he was pleased when she placed him upon her nipple. He thought to kiss her through the fabric, but he rapidly swayed away from patience, and instead pulled on the silk. A button popped, pinging against his chest.

Jane gripped his shirt at his hips and pulled him to her. The damage went unremarked, so he tugged the fabric again, popping out another fragile button from the few loose threads that had once held it.

The taste of her, hard and tight in his mouth, combined with the salt and lilac scent of her desire and with the infuriatingly calm pace of her pulse, he found he could not stop. There was so much here to behold, to inspect and devour, and yet, he felt quite satisfied with this small taste. For now.

"That's an amazing kiss," she whispered. "Do the other."

"You're quite the bossy lover," he murmured, but then tore away the shirt from her other breast and moistened it quickly, followed by a long, rolling suck.

"We're not lovers."

"We will be soon enough." Michael twined both hands into her wild hair and looked down at her. "Right now, Jane. Let's not stop."

"But—"

"It's good that we don't know anything about each other. It's exciting. It gets me hard. Feel me."

He shifted against her hip and Jane lifted her thigh to snuggle against his erection. The friction rocketed all sensation to that one erotic spot. The world began there. *So close to coming.*

Yet, *how* the world ended, could only conclude with a bite.

"Oh, Michael, I'm not sure."

"Don't refuse me, Jane." Just a little persuasion. That's all she needed. But before he could even tap her thoughts, her silent nod bested that ulterior plan.

"Let's go to the bedroom," she said, and tugging him along, she sped down the hallway.

Chapter 8

He'd not intended to exile himself with a beautiful woman, and then make her his love slave. But things were progressing in that direction. Enslavement would take more than a few kisses, but it had a nice ring to it, didn't it?

It is what he did well, and enjoyed—making love. Yet, it had been a while since he'd *indulged* in the act. Sex and blood, they went together like salt and pepper. And yet, some ridiculously confident part of him had convinced his conscience that he could actually do this *without* biting Jane.

Of course that was sensible. He needed to keep his secret from her.

Because if she did find out, she would either leave

in a fit of alarm, or be dead. Those were the only two options, because remaining in the house with a vampire didn't—and shouldn't—make sense to any mortal.

Sure, he could enthrall her following the bite, clearing her memory of the event, but there would remain a telling bruise. Jane would write the first one off as a hickey, gained during the heat of passion. But he would do it again. And again. He knew himself. Once was never enough.

So, if this were to work, Michael had to at least *attempt* restraint.

And should he not succeed, at least he'd given it the old college try. Michael had never attended college, but who could think of education when a half naked woman was kneeling on the bed, holding her arms out to him?

Lilacs spumed out from a tub on the counter in front of the windows. Combined with the sultry evening breeze through the open sash, the room oozed coyly with the sweet floral perfume. It briefly masked the hot crimson scent of Jane's blood—a boon to Michael's self control. But too quickly, her perfume invaded his senses and crept into his veins.

Stripping off his shirt, he stood in the suede pants that fastened with buttons instead of a zipper. The seams were studded with grommets below the knees. Stage wear, but that was all he owned.

"You're more of a vixen than I'd originally thought." He flicked the top button of his pants open.

"I suppose you prefer your women this way?" She leaned back on the bed. The pajama top splayed completely open and her breasts sat high. Pale flesh glistened like moonlight. Perfect handfuls. They tasted good, too. "I've never had sex with a rock star. Does this make me a groupie?"

"Let's not even go there, Jane. I've already explained I don't have *women*." He leaned over her and stroked his tongue over her nipple. Soundly. And again, for good measure. "Slip down your bottoms, Jane sweet. Let's get you comfortable."

"You first," she purred. "I think your pants are too tight, and mighty uncomfortable."

Two more flicks, released his pants, and Michael shimmied them down to the floor. He kicked off his boots and then crawled over to the woman laying in wait on the bed.

Gripping the thin pajama bottoms, he tugged them down.

Dipping his tongue into her navel, he vacillated on whether to venture north or south. The rush of her blood increased in his brain, and he was now aware of her pulse beats beneath his tongue.

His canines tingled. Yes, even having sated his thirst, the reaction to arousal could not be avoided. Damn it. And he'd so hoped to indulge in all that her body could offer, not just the liquid treat of her blood.

"Michael?"

Sliding his fingers between her legs, he tested what he knew he wouldn't have opportunity to enjoy. "So hot," he whimpered. "I—"

Wrenching his neck to the side, he winced and

swore inwardly as his fangs completely descended. Wanting heartbeats pounded between his ears, becoming louder than the instruments his band members played on stage. And this beat, while musical, attracted none but the monster.

"Leave!"

"What?"

"Did you hear me?" He gnashed his teeth at her. No hiding the long white fangs. "It's not safe. Lock yourself in another room."

Blood. Hot. Drink.

The monster needed to be appeased.

And yet, the fear he expected—why, the very drug he craved—did not rise in the blood that flowed beneath his touch.

Jane knelt up, eyeing his deadly fangs. The faery tales in her eyes spoke of grim dealings.

"Listen to me, Jane. Get out of here!"

The vampire lunged and caught her by the shoulders. Silk tore. The shirt fluttered to the bed. So strong, this urge. It clawed. It growled. The body had been teased toward satisfaction.

Now it was time for the real hunger.

"You're a—" She reached for his mouth.

To touch his fangs? Michael slapped away her hand. What kind of woman was this?

"Don't touch me," he growled and shook her by the shoulders. "I will warn you once. If you leave now—"

"But you're a vampire," she exclaimed, so casually, he might have thought she'd just announced a sunny day. "How could I have missed it?"

"What?" Michael's hunger suddenly took a whack from left field. "Missed it?"

He shoved her away from him, and stood back. His pants still around his ankles, he pulled them up and turned from her. Stomping out a pace before the bed, he flexed his fists, unable to pinpoint the exact emotion he should be feeling. Rage, anger, disappointment? Everything was wrong. What the hell?

He kicked the wall above the baseboard. It felt good. So he did it again. The only way to redirect the need was through pain.

Kick the monster away. Get it out from his body! Why could he not just enjoy a woman?

Jane cleared her throat, which drew Michael from the compulsive kicking.

"I should have noticed the shimmer when we touched," she said. "And yet, I thought it merely the weird excitement of you kissing me. It's been so long— Well, not that long. Oh, Michael, we need to talk."

This was not right. Jane should not be sitting there on the bed, her breasts bared and her attitude so— so nonchalant! She should be screaming. Yes? It was all about the scream.

And if he could no longer invoke the scream by flashing his fangs, well then—he wasn't having it— he *could* make her scream. And he would.

Lunging for the woman on the bed, Michael fit his hands to her head, pushing her back into the thick coverlet and pinning her legs with his knees.

Fangs tearing across his bottom lip, he opened his mouth wide.

Yes, do it. Take her. Feed me.

He wasn't going to dance around this any longer. Exile? What for? If the monster wanted the kill, then he'd take it.

"No, Michael!"

As he lunged in to bite, Jane managed to twist out of his grasp. Her hair tangled in his fingers, but he couldn't grip it fast enough to stop her retreat.

"Come back here," he growled. "It won't hurt, I promise. Give yourself to the persuasion, Jane. It can be so good for you."

"No, you can't!"

"I can take whatever I wish from you." He shoved her down again, and crawled over her body. *Yes, look at the fangs, you. Be afraid, be very afraid.* "You are too weak to fight me. Now stop trying to get away."

She kneed him in the groin. He winced, but it affected him little. The need overwhelmed anything else he felt. The scent of her frenzied him. Jane's pulse filled his veins and tromped through his head. She was everywhere.

"You don't want to die," she managed, "not this way."

"Unless you've a stake, I don't think I'll be treading the grave this night." He tugged on her nipple, hoping to draw her from the protest and back into arousal, and yet, if only he could push this skirmish to real fear. "I can hurt you, Jane. I will hurt you if you do not obey."

Pinning down her wrists near her shoulder, Michael lunged in for her neck. As he tasted her skin, so taunt against her throat, he closed his eyes to the exquisite experience of breaking virgin flesh. Every part of him craved the blood. Adrenaline coursed through his body, stinging his every nerve ending with an erotic stab. He never denied himself a thing.

Tonight would be no different.

"I'm a witch," he heard her mutter.

And like that, his fangs retracted.

Chapter 9

"Not exactly a witch, but witch's blood runs in my veins."

Michael eased a hand alongside his crotch. He ached, and needed satisfaction—both sex and blood. But he was no fool.

Pushing off the bed, he swung back into the pace, stomping some because it just needed to be done.

"Not a witch, but you have witch's blood? What kind of story are you playing, Jane? If you don't want to have sex—"

"Sex? You were going to bite me!"

"It's a part of sex!" He beat the wall behind him with a fist. Kicking and beating on things always alleviated the frustration, but he was pretty sure no amount of physical destruction was going to simmer it tonight.

"I'm serious," Jane said. "My blood is poison to vampires. And look at you. A vampire! This is completely nuts."

She thought so? It wasn't every day he tried to bite into a succulent neck and the victim screamed 'witch!' "How do you know about vamps and witches?"

"Sit down."

He crossed his arms over his chest. "I prefer to stand."

"All right." She tugged her top shut and when she fingered the empty buttonholes, Michael quickly said, "No. Leave it. You can talk like that."

She bristled at his demand, but, after running a finger along the open hem of the shirt, she left it as it was. Though her hair spilled over her shoulders and down her chest, her breasts were revealed, the rosy curve of a ruched aureole showing on the one side.

Michael folded a leg and sat on the edge of the bed. Because he needed to hear this. And, it was difficult to stand too far from the one thing he wanted to dive into. Yes, he still wanted what the monster needed.

"You're a witch?"

The desire to push her back onto the bed and tear off her clothes struggled with his need to listen. There was nothing to stop him from taking her.

Except the truth.

"My birth name is Jeanne Rénan," she said, pronouncing her first name with a French accent and making it sound like *Zhaun*.

Hell, another bloody Frenchwoman?

Michael had spent some time in France. The one great love of his life had been French. But he hadn't picked up the French tinge to Jane's voice. Make that Zhaun.

"My father, vicomte Baptiste Rénan, is a vampire."

She pressed a finger to his lips as a huff of breath expelled from his chest. "There's more. My mother's name is Roxane Desrues, and she is a witch. Remember when I told you I was born in '81?"

He nodded silently, taking it all in. A witch and a vampire as parents?

"I was born in *eighteen* eighty-one, in the city of Paris. I am neither a witch, nor a vampire. I can sense magic when there is a witch present, but I can't perform magic, speak a spell or cast a charm. Though, there is magic within me. The world often reacts to that magic, which you may have already noticed. Your mood lifts when I'm around?"

He nodded. "When first meeting you I— Hell, is that why I've been so attracted to you?"

"That's simply your body reacting to what it wants from me. Vampires are compelled to witch's blood, I'm sure you know."

Yes, but also compelled to their death, for witch's blood was poison to a vampire. Bloody hell, he'd been but a stab of his tooth away—from death.

"And, thanks to my father's blood coursing through my veins, I can feel a vampire through the shimmer common only to another vampire. Though, it didn't occur to me that sexual arousal also feels much like the shimmer."

She looked confused. This night was becoming a nightmare.

"I've walked this earth for one hundred and twenty-five years, Michael. And you are the first vampire I have ever kissed. That is…if you don't count kissing my father on the cheek."

He deserved credit for holding his jaw in place, and not dropping it to the floor. A struggle between amazement and horror worked at him. Clenching his fingers into claws, he tensed them, watching the veins pop.

"I've an uncle, on my mother's side, who is a—"

"Warlock?" Michael tried.

"No, male witches are not common in my family. The magic tends to leave the men alone. Besides, a warlock is a traitor, not a witch. Anyway, my uncle Damien is a vampire too, thanks to both my mother and father. The entire tale is long and a little twisted. Suffice to say, I've grown up in the company of supernatural beings."

"Which is why you're not afraid of me."

"Not at all. And I know that frustrates you. You crave the adrenaline, yes?"

"You know too much…" he murmured.

"It's a guess. Were you trying to frighten me the other day when you leapt out from the hallway?"

Wisely, Michael remained silent on that little incident.

"Well, you did scare me, but I've this reaction to fear that sends me giggling. Might be because of my upbringing. If your relatives are vampires and witches, there isn't much that can scare a person. I mean really scare me. Though elves can do it with ease."

Elves? In all his years, he never met, let alone heard, of an elf.

Michael pressed his palms onto the bed behind him and leaned back, away from her. It felt so far a distance. He wanted Jane back upon his lips. There, at his mouth. His. For good or for the very worst.

And yet, how could he even imagine touching her again? They were not meant to be anywhere near one another. True witch or not, if she spoke the truth, and witch's blood ran through her veins, she was poison to him.

"We're enemies" is all he said.

Witches and vampires had never mixed, and the witch—while offering some pretty extreme boons to the vampire—such an offer came with a deadly price tag. Death by blood.

Michael had never met a witch before, but he knew enough to avoid them like the black plague.

He abruptly stepped off the bed and paced toward the windows. Below him a thick bouquet of lilacs gave off a deceptively innocent fragrance.

"You tell me true?" He glanced over his shoulder. Jane still sat on the bed, a porcelain doll on the vast piece of furniture. This time she didn't wield a knife, yet her words cut him just as deeply. "You had no idea what I was?"

"Of course not. I would have never allowed things to go this far had I known."

"Really? And yet you say you can recognize the shimmer. That sensation only another vampire can feel when he touches his own kind? I've touched you before tonight. You must have known. Maybe that's what you wanted? To lure the vampire into your sexual trap and then—*bang*— one bite and you've claimed yet another prize to your belt."

"Yet another? What are you saying? That I'm a slayer? Michael, I had no idea. And you must admit it is rare one of the dark holds such a public position."

The dark. It is what the witches called the vampires. And they, in turn, called themselves *the light.* Bullshit. Anything that could bring his death with a tiny drop of blood was nothing but bad, no light involved whatsoever.

The muscles in his arms flexed as he wrenched them back and forth before him, working out his unsettled aggressions. What to do with her now? The game plan had been completely crossed over and scribbled up into a fine mess.

He paced before the window, unwilling to return to the bed. She seemed docile enough, but it may be the witch's way. But he wasn't going to run. No, that wasn't his style. Facing down a challenge and showing it his teeth—now that's the way he lived his life.

Like he'd shown the monster his teeth?

"So let me get this straight. You're not a vampire, though, your father is?"

"I have never craved blood, nor do I need it to survive, as I know all vampires are wont."

"Have you ever been bitten?"

"Once, by my uncle. That is how we came to learn I'm not pre-destined to vamp out."

If he attempted to put a logical spin to her confession he'd never succeed. A child born of a witch and a vampire. How was that even possible? Without the sharing of blood, no vampire could ever truly commit to his mate. Blood was the world. Procreation did not come about without making love *and* the blood.

"And not a witch," he said. His words were quiet, thought through before he voiced them. "But your mother is? Does she cast spells and ride a broomstick?"

"No broomsticks, but certainly plenty of spells. Witches aren't what you see at Halloween. She doesn't cackle over her cauldron or worship the devil."

"I know that. I'm not an idiot."

"Our lineage traces back to Druidic times. There is true magic in my mother. She was born that way. Only I cannot command it, as my mother does."

Michael nodded, taking it in.

"I wish I could. I've tried, believe me."

"To be a witch?"

"To tap into the innate magic within me. I'm cursed to forever walk the line between the two."

"Have you never wished for the vampirism?"

"No," she said in a dreamy sigh-like manner. "I've always related to my mother more than my father."

What luxury, to have both parents. Michael had

not a father to relate to, for he'd left his mother to go to war before Michael had been born. World War II. His boots and dog tags had arrived in a small box on the eve of Michael's fifth birthday.

"I have their immortality," Jane offered. "Though that was in part due to a ritual my mother and father insisted I partake of when I was in my twenties."

Interesting. "So you weren't born immortal?"

Jane rested her elbows on the foot of the bed frame behind her. Her nudity completely forgotten, she could not be aware of how alluring she was to him—or how frustrating.

"Not sure," she replied. "How does one know such a thing unless it has occurred before and been documented? My father insists his daughter live a long life, and he is ever troubled I should die before him. So my parents encouraged me to take steps to ensure it would be so. I've the skin and strong bone structure of a twenty-year-old woman, yet my mind is very old."

"An old soul," Michael said. "I've always imagined you otherworldly. Not of this realm. And now here you are, peeling back your mask."

"I didn't wear it to hide from you. If anyone was hiding something—"

He put up a palm to stop her. "We've both had secrets. I don't normally come out and introduce myself as a vampire to everyone I meet. It's unnecessary, and frankly, dangerous. You, of all people, should understand that."

"I do. But then I have to wonder, just now, you were

going to bite me. And then what? Toss me aside after you'd enthralled the memory from me? Kill me?"

"No!" He fisted the air. "Don't ever accuse me of that, Jane. That is not something I will do. Ever." And yet, that last word came out as but a whisper.

"I'm glad," she said. "That puts you leagues ahead of the majority of the dark."

"Not that I'm incapable of it, mind you. I could snap your neck before you had a thought to bite your lip and spit at me, know that, witch."

"I'm not a witch, Michael, but..." Her sigh rifled across his bare back.

Michael flexed his shoulders, working at the stinging ache that rose between his pecs. "But what?"

"When my uncle bit me, that was the first time we realized I wouldn't change. But my uncle is also immune to witch's blood, because his sister was significant in transforming him. And we've never chanced upon a vampire who would agree to test the theory of my blood being poisonous. So I don't know if my blood *is* deadly to a vampire. I can never know, until it is too late."

"Why don't you kidnap an idiot vamp off the street and test it?"

"Oh, Michael, that's awful. I'd rather *not* know than harm an innocent."

"Which means, no blood from you for me." Michael sighed.

Jane wandered to the doorway to stand, back propped and legs stretched before her. He paced the floor, not sure what to say. There wasn't anything *to* say. He stopped before the bed. The impression of her body lumped the comforter. Her lingering scent drew him down, so he lay back on the bed and crossed his legs at the ankle. The warmth of her crept into him on a sigh.

The ache in his gut certainly was not the blood hunger. Rather the monster stood in the corner now, tail between its legs, cowering at this new information. But Michael wasn't about to cower.

"I've a walking death cocktail sharing my home," he muttered. "Way to chill the libido, Jane."

"It's not my problem, Michael. If you can't control the urge to bite me when we become intimate, then deal with it. I'm fine either way."

"You're fine because you've nothing to risk!"

"*I* almost had sex with a bloody vampire," she raged.

He had never suspected anything strange about Jane. Just thought her a natural beauty in touch with nature and a bit of a fuddy-duddy behind the thick plastic safety glasses. And gorgeous. Hell, why were the gorgeous ones always the most troublesome? "So, you're not keen on vampires? But if your father is one...?"

"I didn't say I'm not keen on them, I've just... never been with a vampire before. As you can imagine, it's not every day a vampire engages a witch in small talk that then leads to having sex."

No, but once, long ago—thousand of years— witches and vampires had been allies. Until the vampires had begun to enslave the witches for the strength and power having sex with them could give them. And to drink their blood? Then the vampire could take the witch's very magic into him, and use it to cast spells. As the witches began to protest, a war broke out. Many more witches died than vampires. And so a great Protection spell had been cast to ensure all witches' blood worked like poison to the vampire. The two factions had been enemies since.

"Yes, we were so close. And yet, you stopped me." He turned onto his elbow and studied the porcelain doll propped in the doorway. "You could have let me go on with it. Then you would have known for sure the effects of your blood. We may have continued to have sex, I would have bitten you—no dead vampire. Or, you could have learned you've most powerful death in your veins. You resisted the opportunity."

She shrugged. "Clean-up would have been a bitch."

Michael smirked. He couldn't help himself. He shouldn't find that comment at all amusing. The levity was welcome.

And that was her skill, wasn't it? Jane had the ability to lighten him, to make him step back and take a look at the world in new ways. Was it the magic within that she'd said made others react to her?

The idea of being controlled by magic, without his permission, didn't sit well with him. Though, if she had no control over it…

Closing his eyes, Michael listened to the beat of Jane's life. Constant, her heartbeats. She had entered him. And even with this devastating information about her, he honestly didn't want to push her out of his blood.

She is light. Take it!

He lunged off the bed and stepped over to embrace her. It felt right moving into her space, touching her.

"What are you doing?" she asked.

"I'm not sure."

Gliding his hands through her hair, he leaned in and drew upon the intoxicating aura of Jane. Yes, inviting, not a bit changed since he'd learned she was the enemy. Still composed of lilacs and cherry wine.

He felt…invigorated, actually. Almost *stronger* than before he'd begun this day. He'd not realized it until now, but he felt a buzz, like he did when he walked off stage and the adrenaline raced through his veins.

Was it because of Jane? Because he so boldly challenged death by now embracing it?

"Please, don't stand so close," she murmured. But her actions were opposite as she clung to his hips. "Nothing's changed, Michael. I still want you. But it would be dangerous. We can't risk it. *You* can't risk it."

Thinking of his safety, was she? Jane was like one of those huge round windows in Notre Dame. So exquisitely complicated.

"Shouldn't that be *my* choice?" He tested the

waters with a quick kiss to her lips. The monster did not stir, but it stood there, in the shadows, observing. "Jane, I won't hurt you, but— Do you have a cross?"

"What? I—no. I don't subscribe to that religious symbol. Crosses were basically banned from the house when I was growing up. I wouldn't use one against you anyway."

"Just a little one. It's all you need. You don't need to believe in it, all that matters is I once believed and was baptized."

"No, absolutely not. You're not thinking right, Michael. Is it the blood hunger? Are you dizzied by the pull of my blood?"

"Oh, Jane, I *can* control the hunger, I'll have you know."

"Then why the exile? I'm guessing you didn't walk away from the spotlight to spend the summer gardening. Why are you here, Michael?"

"There is a reason. I'm…" Could he tell her? Sure, he'd been the one to force them out of their roles as strangers, but this was more intimate than sex, this sharing of one's personal ordeals. "Do I have to tell?"

"No." She tilted a look up into his eyes. Dark emeralds flashed faery tales. A smile softened his dread.

"So it's magic that makes me want to be near you, to stand so close I might become you?" He could understand that.

"It could be. I know vampires can take away magic

by having sex with a witch, and that they are compelled by that same magic to the scent of their blood."

"A wicked spell upon our kind."

"Do you think it's any easier for a woman who isn't a witch, but wants a man who must be wary of her?"

"Oh, Jane."

Their kiss was tender at first, but as she pulled him to her they both deepened the urgency. This felt right.

To hell with you, Michael mentally screamed to the monster. This woman gave him light. And what better person to stand at his side while he struggled to obtain that light than one who understood him because she had lived with his kind?

"So you've nothing against vampires?" he whispered. Her lashes fluttered upon his lips. He dashed out his tongue, but tasted only air.

"There are good and bad vampires, just as there are good and bad mortals. I get along with most anyone if they're respectful to me. What about you? How does sharing a house with a not-quite-witch feel to you? Kinda crawly?"

"Truth? A little. One thin cut to your finger, and if I'm anywhere in the vicinity, well—"

He wanted her desperately. Holding her fed a hunger for that which he'd been unable to control, the wild, the outrageous, and the darkly sensuous. He wanted to take her into his body and lose himself. He wanted to do wild, desperate things that consenting adults did behind closed doors.

How to kiss Jane and make love to her without inviting the monster? Why worry? She knew about him now; she shouldn't flinch at his fangs or his insistent needs.

Death cocktail, remember?

Right. That little detail twisted everything into a complex knot.

A kiss to her chin. The taste of her—cherry wine and lilacs—wilded his heart. Like no other. Death might be worth having sex with this woman.

Sliding a hand beneath her breast, he explored the soft undercurve, daring a stroke across her nipple. The thin shirt was still open and made it easy to feel the pebbled texture. How women, in all their softness, could be so hard, never ceased to astound him. He squeezed.

The sound of Jane's pleasure sang to Michael's soul. Her song cooed him to the edge of control, coaxing with a wanting chorus and the soft harmony of the forbidden. His teeth tingled. The wild in him stalked to the surface. *Crazy red wild need.*

Blood scent called to the monster.

He pushed away from her and stomped to the center of the room. The seductive silence screamed at his insecurities. Standing there, he felt at his teeth, so sharp when he wasn't aware.

"This is not going to work, Jane. Every time I touch you the need to kiss you—to merely *connect* with you—becomes so dark. I want you so fiercely, but I won't hurt you." Gesturing incomprehensibly, he declared, "I *can't* hurt you. It might destroy me."

Michael sighed but then said, "I didn't mean that. Not hurt, but..." *Bite.* "You know I've only heard the tales. What really happens when a vampire drinks witch blood?"

Slipping her tongue out to taste the remnants of his kiss, Jane then tucked her hair behind her ear. Wicked green eyes shone a defiant call to the fallen angel.

"I've only witnessed it once, mind you," she said, "and it wasn't caused by me. Once the witch's blood enters the vampire's system, well...it..."

"Dead vampire?"

"Desiccated vampire, to be exact. The vampire sort of...melts away from the inside and then... explodes."

"Ah. Well, then." Michael clasped his arms tight across his chest. "Such joys to look forward to should I taste your blood." He kicked the bedpost. "Why is it the only woman in the world I want to hold close is the one who could be my death? What kind of karma is this? Not that I don't deserve it."

But did he? Did he really?

"You want to simply hold me?"

"Yes." He breathed lowly. He held out his arms, but didn't move to embrace her. Because he didn't want to break her, or to be broken in return.

"Sometimes—most of the time—I want to hold you. I want to kiss you. I want to—hell, I want to have sex with you, Jane. I want to strip off that silk shirt and taste your breasts that feel like heaven in my hands and bury my face in your hair and just be in you until the both of us can't tell where one ends and the other begins."

"Sounds marvelous."

"It does, doesn't it?" He smacked a fist into his palm. "Bitch that I can't control the blood hunger over my demanding lust. That's what this inner fight is all about. The reason I've secluded myself. I need to get it under control before the press catches wind of my indiscretions."

He paced the floor before Jane. "It used to be I'd kiss a woman, or have sex with her, and then the hunger would demand I drink her blood. Now? I don't get that far. I kiss. I don't have time to think about sex because the monster wants its fill. Immediately. It's like the whole sex blood feed thing has gotten twisted into one of those Gordian knots. I should be able to separate the necessity of blood from the luxury of sex. I should, but I can't."

"So every woman you've been sexually attracted to, you...?"

"Bite her. Makes it difficult to have a relationship, let alone make a simple connection."

And that is what he craved, the comfort of a relationship, of connecting with another, and knowing there was one other person in this world who accepted and understood him. Because while the world perceived his as an idol adored by masses of zealous fans, Michael knew, when on stage, he stood alone. So alone.

"So," Jane said, "if you could learn to control the hunger, we could make love."

He flinched. "I'll never hurt you, Jane. I promise you. But the dark in me isn't privy to the promises made by the light."

"I would never ask you to do something you didn't want to do."

"Making love is not on that Don't Want list. I want, Jane, I want so much— Please, don't touch me. Please, Jane. It's so... My tooth."

He turned from her. His fangs had descended. He wasn't comfortable with closing his mouth completely over the sharp weapons.

"I need to get away from you. Just for now. It's not because I don't want you."

"I understand."

"I'll see you tomorrow night."

"I look forward to it."

And so did he.

Chapter 10

On the one hand, she should be thrilled. A source! And living in the same house as she. The promise of a secure future stood so close, why, it literally embraced her. No need to rely on Ravin Crosse; this matter had taken care of itself.

On the other hand... Did there have to be another hand?

Jane pushed her fingers through her hair as she paced the hallway toward the living room. "I'm sharing a house with a vampire!"

Certainly she wasn't your average woman. Vampires were myth; your average citizen played into the act, but could never quite step over the edge to belief. Though she'd been raised in a household with a witch and a vampire, Jane tended to walk a wide path around it; she'd become as anesthetized by the media as everyone else. Vampires were so popular nowadays they were absolutely commonplace. Everyone wanted to be one. No one really believed in them. And yet, that was the vampire's greatest coup: that they could flaunt themselves publicly, and the world thought it merely a costume or publicity stunt.

But Jane knew better. And so did Michael.

And what was so different about this situation than having lived with a vampire as her father?

Plenty. Namely, that she was still attracted to Michael, even knowing their coming together could prove volatile, if not deadly, to him. He had tried not to show it, but he was concerned. He had to be.

So when he'd asked for space, she'd agreed. Time she needed as well, because suddenly the choices life offered had become so twisted.

Striding into the living room, she plopped onto the covered sofa and caught her head in her hands.

"It wasn't stupid," she said. Not recognizing the truth standing right before her. Twisting the shimmer into sexual desire instead of taking it for what it had been. "Just…oh!"

She had succumbed to surface seduction. And now, she knew what lay beneath the surface was not for her.

"No vampires," she said sternly. "They're not—not what I want. I just want to be normal."

Did she? Because she'd done normal for so long

now, and always that reminder that she could never be normal stabbed at her. The inner magic her mother warned her not to fear teased at her. She wanted to control it. Over the years she had attempted to master her latent magic, and not once had she succeeded.

Jane's sigh lifted her shoulders. She rolled onto her side and propped her head on the arm of the couch, curling up her legs to her stomach.

To have considered Michael Lynsay as a romantic prospect had been a bad choice. Yet strangely, a comfortable one.

It was high noon, and Michael didn't feel like sleeping. The recording studio didn't call to him, though he had promised Jesse he'd go over the tracks to a few songs The Fallen was working on. The lyrics needed reshaping. But for that he needed his iPod, in which he'd stored the files on the hard drive.

Where had he lost that? Was some kid going through the files right now? He'd be the neighborhood star the moment he shared the unreleased video with his friends.

The record company would have his head if that video got into the wrong hands. It wasn't Michael's job to have to worry about things like that.

Hand him a microphone and let him rock. That was Michael's role in the greater scheme of things. If he couldn't sing—ah, hell, he didn't want to consider life without music. It provided a necessary counterbalance to the dark.

Much as music was his everything, he didn't feel it today. The only beat he wanted to play with was the one beneath Jane's flesh. Skin so soft and creamy he could lick her all night and never grow full of her taste.

This distraction thing seemed to be key to not thinking about the reason he was here. Which was good. He hadn't fed for over twenty-four hours, which was remarkable. Though, it wasn't the need for blood that troubled him. He'd gone for almost a week if The Fallen's concerts were back to back. Performing on stage gave him the same adrenaline rush the fear did.

So where was Jane?

Not a witch, but witch's blood in her veins? Damn.

"This is stupid." He shrugged a T-shirt over his head and arms, and paced out of the bathroom to find Jane. "Enough brooding. And I'm not afraid of her. No slip of a woman is going to keep me away. Witch or not."

She wasn't in the workroom. The first window was complete, and stood propped against one of the original windows. Vibrant colors beamed across the floor, stretching up to the door where Michael glanced in. The sun was bright today.

Jane wasn't in the kitchen, and the rest of the house was bare of furniture so he didn't bother to check the other rooms. Glancing out the window over the sink he spied Jane's fluttering blue skirts— or rather she slashed wildly at something.

"What the hell?"

A storm of insects buzzed about Jane's head. She batted and punched at them.

Michael took off in a run out the back door. As he got closer he could make out the yellow and black bodies. They were bees. Probably a dozen of the big fat bumblebee kind.

"Jane, don't slash at them! They won't sting!"

"Oh, yes they will!" she shouted, and continued to bat at the angry insects. "They won't leave me alone. Oh, Michael make them go away!"

Not sure how to scare off something so small, and seeing Jane's frantic arm movements were doing little to ward off the things, Michael tore his T-shirt over his head and flapped it at the bees. The wave of fabric beat half a dozen back, but they zoomed right back at Jane. One crawled in her hair. Another on her shoulder.

He winced, feeling as if he'd been stung. But the fat ones like this didn't sting, did they?

Just above his eye it burned—and then he realized what he'd done. The sun was high. He shouldn't be outside.

He had to get out of the sun. But not without Jane.

"Damn it!" He grasped a bee and squeezed, dropping it dead to the grass. A few more snatches served the same result.

The corner of his eyes watered and burned. His right shoulder burned.

"Jane, let me cover your head." He fit the T-shirt over her hair and then whisked her under his arm. "Run with me!"

Batting away the insistent bees, he made it to the house and shoved Jane inside. Smacking a bee against the wall, it stuck there.

"Are they gone?" she cried, still under the shirt. "Michael?"

A woozy rush swirled through his brain. Michael staggered. Sunburned so quickly? He felt his brow. The flesh was open and burnt.

"Oh, *mon Dieu.*" Jane pulled away the shirt and gaped at Michael's face. "You're burned. Michael, the sun, why did you do that?"

"You were in trouble. What the hell got into those bees?"

"I don't know. I've always attracted nature, plants and birds and such, but they've never attacked me like that. No, they weren't attacking, it was more like they wanted to be near me—oh, but who cares about that. You need medical attention."

"Right. Call the ambulance and admit one vampire." She touched his face, but he jerked away. His ego had taken a harder beating than his body. "I'm fine."

"No, you're not. The flesh is oozing. I didn't bring along any first aid, save some aspirins, but I can mix up something with the catmint outside the window. Come into the kitchen. Maybe some ice will help while I prepare a cream."

Upon discovery of a few red welts on Jane's neck, Michael insisted she care for herself first.

After she'd mounded some moist salt to the

stings, Jane then began to mix a cream for Michael's burns.

He would heal. In a few days. The burns had eaten away the surface of his flesh to reveal oozing red beneath. Above his eyes and on his shoulder. He'd been burned by the sun once before, and he'd vowed never to let it happen again. Then, he'd been a new vampire, and the arm he'd stretched along the open car window as he'd driven through town during high noon had taken three days to completely heal.

But now he couldn't be bothered for his own well-being. All that mattered is that Jane was safe.

Bees? What a weird thing.

"Hold still."

She had mixed up something not entirely bad smelling, and now scooped some out with her finger.

"How long do I have to wear that stuff? It's green, Jane. Seriously, I'll heal."

"This might make the healing go faster. If anything, it'll soothe. Doesn't it hurt?"

He shrugged. Yes, it hurt. "No. I'm fine."

"Oh, Michael. Please?"

He wrapped an arm around her waist and pulled her down to sit on his lap. The green stuff on her finger wavered under his nose, and smelled minty, and tangy.

"See, it's not so bad."

"Just a little then." He closed his eyes as she tenderly smoothed over the burns above his right temple. The damage stretched down the side of his face to mid cheek and there was a spot on the side of his nose. It hurt when she touched him. Like the mortal pain he had not experienced for decades. And he didn't want to ever experience it again.

He shoved away her hand. "Kiss me."

"But I'm not finished. Your shoulder…"

"Jane, I asked a simple favor. I honestly believe a kiss will do more for my aches than that smelly cream. My lips are not burned."

She touched his mouth with hers. So gentle. Like a bee glancing against him. Friendly bees that had wanted to be near her? Must be the magic.

Michael knew very well that if a vampire had sex with a witch he could draw on her magic. And what would that magic do for the vampire? It wouldn't allow him to perform a spell or cast a charm—blood was required for that—but it would make him stronger. Perhaps, make him heal faster?

"If you want to help me," he said, sliding a hand up under her shirt and cupping her breast. "We need to have sex."

"What? Oh. You mean…"

"It's supposed to give the vampire strength, more power, to make love with a witch."

"Well, I'm not—" She bowed her head, suddenly blushingly shy. "You think it would work with a not-quite-witch?"

"I'm willing to give it a try."

She shrugged a hand through her tousled hair and blew at a rogue strand. "I don't know."

"I promise to behave this time."

"It's not that. I feel a mess after that bizarre encounter. I want to take a shower. Why don't you meet me up there?"

"I'm right behind you."

Michael had rescued her from that ridiculous battle with the bees, without thought for his own safety. He could have been burned much more severely, for it only took a few minutes for the sun to work its devastation to a vampire's flesh.

She liked to consider that a man had come to her rescue. Like a knight in shining armor—no, she didn't need the knight. Nor was a white stallion required to gallop such a man into her life. What she needed was someone who would accept her for what she was, in all her bizarreness— armor optional.

Michael seemed to be that man. But she didn't want to rush to conclusions. For now, the adventure of taking a lover suited her just fine.

Jane switched on the shower and stripped off her skirt and top, leaving them in a heap upon the toilet seat. Within seconds the hot water began to steam up the room, streaking the mirror. Stepping inside the stall, she wet her hair.

She knew the legend Michael had referred to. Vampires had once been able to take a witch's magic into them during the act of making love, a magic that would increase their strength. They had also once been able to drink witch's blood, which gave them the same abilities the witch had. Witch magic. Those vampires who had earned—or rather, stolen—the magic were called *bewitched;* and they were revered by their own kind for it.

But the vampires greed to gain more and more power through the stolen magic prompted the Protection, and witch blood became poisonous to vampires. They could still give their magic during sex, but what vampire would risk that?

To this day, only a handful of the ancient *bewitched* vampires survived. Or so Jane had been told. There was no evidence to be found of the ancients.

That Jane's parents had coexisted peacefully had never given her a fear of the vampire. The only thing she truly feared was if Michael could not control the blood hunger.

She'd take that chance. Because she wanted him.

Glass doors closed off the double-wide shower. Michael's body slid up behind hers. She hadn't even heard him enter the bathroom but his presence did not frighten her. Strong hands skated down her slick forearms. Yet dry, his hair tickled over her shoulder. He kissed the crown of her head.

"Thank you," Jane murmured. "It was so silly, but they scared me."

"Attracted to your magic?"

"I think so."

His hand swept around the curve of her hip, gliding up her stomach and cupped her breast. Possessed, she, and happy for it. "Like me," he murmured against her ear. "I am attracted to you."

She wanted him to hold her so closely, where one

ended and the other began became a blur. He kissed the side of her neck. The hard lines of his body eased against her shoulders, her hips, and her thighs. The length of his erection rested at the juncture of her thigh and hip, not demanding, but simply there. A man who wanted. A man who needed. A man she wanted to heal.

"How does it work?" he asked. "The sex magic."

"Not sure."

"There's not a spell you need to speak?"

"It wouldn't work if I tried. I said I couldn't control it, Michael."

"Well, then, we'll have to work at this until we see results."

He tilted up her chin and she opened her mouth over his. They kissed for lost moments in the hot rain. Water splat their faces and slickened their kisses.

He whispered in her ear, "Turn around. Hold the bar."

Jane clasped the steel towel bar.

"You know," he said. He followed the slender curve of her waist, gliding across her stomach. "A vampire usually requires permission to enter private property."

"Yes." A silly quirk that never ceased to startle her when her father had attempted to enter a friend's home without permission. It was one bane against the vampire she couldn't figure out, and yet, though she suspected he was teasing, she admired the suggestion.

Jane leaned back and whispered, "Enter vampire, freely, and of your own will."

No further words were spoken. No directions needed. Michael's fingers slid along her torso. Jane moved to his silent directions, pressing against him and inviting one who should be her natural enemy to take her as he pleased.

With a groan and a firm, controlling clasp against her belly, Michael slid inside her. She moaned at the delicious pleasure of being completely filled. At first he moved slowly, but soon he picked up the tempo and the wanting beat of their need became too much to bear. Jane gasped as she climaxed. And with her, her vampire lover thrust back his head and cried out in release. The swoon captured them both. This music needed no accompaniment.

Dropping his head onto her shoulder, Michael breathed against her neck. "So good. Jane, it worked."

"Are you sure? The burns, have they healed?"

"No, not that. We made love. Without…"

"Oh." Without him biting her.

Turning, she reached down and slicked her hand across his semi-hard erection. A gasping exhale shivered over her lips. "Let's not think about it. If we don't speak of it, we won't summon it."

"Round two?"

She touched the top of his brow, careful not to violate the angry burn. "Let's do it."

"Face to face this time."

He reached up and flipped off the shower. Lifting her up, she wrapped her legs around his hips, and he carried her out into the bedroom. Soaking wet, they landed on the bed in a tumble of limbs.

"Sweet Jane," he moaned as he entered her again. "This is where I belong."

Chapter 11

Michael woke hours later. It was evening. He never slept long when it wasn't in total darkness.

Jane lay on her stomach, gorgeously naked, her pinky finger twined within his hair. She smelled earthy and like sex, salt and dreams. Much as he wanted to linger, to wrap his body about her sweetness and fall into oblivion, there were pressing matters he couldn't ignore.

Sliding carefully off the bed, so as not to wake her, he collected his clothes, which were scattered over the bedroom floor.

Zipping up his pants, he then ducked into the bathroom and flipped on the light. He peered into the mirror, and lifted the hair away from his forehead.

"Well, I'll be."

The burn was gone. As if it had never been there in the first place, and but for the memory of the pain, he'd guess it hadn't been. A twist of his waist revealed the back of his shoulder to him. No burns there either.

"She really does have magic within her."

He touched his skin. Felt right. Like it had never been damaged. A flex of his biceps, and he wondered if he didn't feel stronger. Maybe the muscles were tighter? Like he'd just had a good workout, and yet, he had never in his life worked out.

"I want more," he decided. "If one time with her does this for me, I'll take all the magic I can get."

Jane woke to the scent of beauty. A breeze tickled her bare legs and stomach. She sniffed and something moved across her upper lip. Clawing her fingers into the bed sheets, she dug into something soft, yet moist.

She opened her eyes and smiled. Yellow rose petals covered the sheets, and they were scattered all over her body.

Turning over, she slid her hand across the empty half of the bed. Petals scattered and tickled across her neck.

She stretched her limbs, wishing she could slumber in the petals all day like a lazy sun-drenched cat. But she caught sight of Michael, sitting on the marble counter by the window.

"You've been busy," she murmured. Grasping a

handful of petals, she held them high and let them flutter to her stomach.

"You like them?"

"Do you intend to overwhelm me with flowers on a daily basis?"

He crossed the room and slid sinuously onto the bed beside her. A sexy panther stalking his prey. "Got a problem with that?"

"Not at all." She turned into him and kissed his lower lip. Toothpaste. How wonderfully normal to smell toothpaste on her vampire lover. "What time is it?"

"Evening. We took up the whole afternoon having sex. One, two…"

She gripped his wrist and shook the rose petals from his fingers. "You like to count things?"

He chuckled and ended it with a kiss to her nose. "I've always been a counter. Do you know it took me a good hour to spread these around you? Last count tallied two hundred sixty-two petals."

His eyes strayed to the sheets. "Oh, hell, I can't look at them. I need a distraction."

"Oh *mon Dieu*, it worked!" She stroked his forehead and smoothed that finger down the side of his face.

Michael playfully snapped at her, but then sucked her finger into his mouth. "Sex magic," he said. "I could get used to it."

"I can't believe it. My…magic?"

"Even if you can't control it, it's obviously in there, somewhere. I don't know how it works, but it did and I'm not complaining."

"Wow. So if we continued to…"

"Have sex?"

"Yes. You would get stronger? Maybe become…?"

"Very powerful? Able to leap tall buildings in a single bound? Shall we try again?"

"Michael, I'm not sure. But you did avoid biting me. Do you think that was magic, as well?"

"Jane, let's not try to figure it out. Can't you accept that it happened?"

"Of course. Yes." She kissed him. He smiled so widely, it was truly the first time she'd seen him so elated. Gone was her broody, testy vampire, to be replaced with an eager, hungry man. It was great that he felt he'd benefited from their intimate contact. "But what do I get out of the deal?"

He slid her hand down to his crotch, and waggled his brows.

"You think so, eh big boy?"

A kiss to the crown of each of her breasts seduced her away from her need to have answers. Threading her fingers into his hair, Jane pulled him closer, making sure his mouth landed on her nipple. "Oh, that's good. I like it when you do that, so…oh, lightly."

"You get me, how's that for a deal?" he said.

"It's not magic, but I won't complain."

Michael trickled a few petals over her breasts. "But we can't become complacent. I've been thinking, and it may have just been a fluke."

"Meaning?"

"Meaning, if we make love again—and we will—

and I start to vamp out on you, I want you to run when I tell you to run. Deal?"

"I think I understand the importance of running. Deal. I'd hate to see the results of one drop of my blood touching this gorgeous body of yours. Oh, you smell so good."

"So if you've never seen it happen, how can you really know?" he wondered from the rise of her breast. "Your father teach you all this stuff about vampires?"

"I did grow up with him. I've never known anything else, so it is all quite natural to me."

"Did he ever try to drink your blood?"

"Never! He's quite civilized. A vampire need only take blood once a week or so. Older ones can go for more than a month."

"That's insane."

"No." She sighed and plucked a rose petal and toggled it between two fingers. "That is sane."

"You're saying I'm a freak?"

"That has already been proven." With a smile, she kissed his forehead and nestled onto his shoulder to lie next to him. "You know, European vampires *are* more civilized than American ones."

"Says the French chick."

"I'm serious. The tribes they form here in America are ruthless."

"I've been pretty lucky to avoid the tribes. I fool a lot of my kind, being in front of the spotlight."

"Good for you. Here in the States I've noticed your kind tend to gather forces and, well, they're much like the street gangs. And once the tribes get you in their clutches, you're theirs."

She pushed onto her elbows and tickled him under the chin with a petal. "And then you've got the vigilantes."

"Vigilante vamps?"

"Vigilante witches. I've a friend who stalks the tribes. It is her profession. You need a vampire taken out, you go to her. She's killed too many to count. So you wouldn't want to meet her in a dark alley."

"Duly warned."

She stroked her fingers along the plumpness of his lower lip. The tip of his tongue dashed out, and she poked it back.

"Michael, I'm glad you avoid the tribes. You are an individual. You like to stand before a crowd and drink in the adulation. And I adore you for that. You'll never be the sort to answer to orders or to skulk about with vengeance in his eyes."

"You think so? I suppose I'm not much for skulking."

"It requires avoiding the spotlight."

"You're right. Not for me. So you think there's hope for this blood addict?"

"They say the best way to get over a habit is to replace it with another."

He stroked her mouth with his thumb. "You are a feisty bit of copper and sunshine. Are you suggesting my new addiction is to become a sex magic addict?"

"Maybe."

"I am there."

He kissed her, brushing her lips with his before opening her mouth and running his tongue along her teeth. Not often did he French kiss her, and when he did, it was brief. Jane figured he considered it too dangerous to introduce his teeth into the mix. They were both much safer to keep them tucked away.

"So you've seen your father...you know? Do the deed."

"Never." She tapped his lower lip, nestling a finger into the slight indent in the middle. "Though there was one occasion he came home with blood on his lips. I was very curious because I knew that's what he did to survive, but had never before seen such bold proof of it. Mother yelled at him. It's my uncle who didn't take caution that I wouldn't be exposed to the darker stuff. Well, I've told you, he bit me once."

"You did? I don't remember." Michael propped up onto his elbows. "Jane, if you've been bitten by a vampire, that should mean—"

"The circumstances were very different. Uncle Damien is immune to witch's blood."

"How? If he can be, maybe I can be..."

"It's a long story. I just—should you taste my blood, it could mean a painful death to you. I don't want to risk it, Michael."

"I suppose not."

"You suppose? Michael." She bracketed his jaw. "Repeat after me. Witch's blood. Death cocktail."

"I know, but you're not—"

"My mother's blood runs through my veins. And

she is a witch. Now enough. I'll never let you bite me. So don't even consider it."

"I'm not, but Jane." He sighed and sat up, swinging his legs off the bed. "You need to understand something about me. You and I, if there's to be a you and me… It's all about the blood, you know that. If I can't drink from you—"

"I'm not like all the other women." She sat up and turned. Rose petals stuck to her arms. "You don't need my blood, Michael. You just think you do."

"Jane." He clasped her hand and drew her to sit beside him. The shimmer toyed at her chilly response to his mood. "I *know* I do. This is my truth, so please hear it." As his fingers tickled up her bare arm, she felt she could never be mad at him for a thing. Most especially for something they could, neither of them, completely understand.

"If I never know the taste of your blood," Michael said, "you'll never be a part of me."

"My father has not tasted my blood. We are very close."

"It's a sex thing, Jane. Don't even try to convince me you can't understand that."

She understood. Without the blood the sex wasn't the same. And without sex, the blood meant nothing. And with blood, well, that was Michael's entire world. Didn't she want to be a part of that world?

Yes, you do. So why are you tossing up a wall now?

Because the unknowing wouldn't allow her to relax. And because she had come to this town with a very specific purpose—complete the ritual.

Would Ravin secure a source in time? And even then, if she and Michael got beyond the ritual and thought about having a life together, what kind of weird couple would they make?

Truth was, Michael could never drink her blood. And without that? He may never feel a true connection to her.

She sighed and laid her head on his shoulder. Not sure what to tell him, she closed her eyes and decided the moment didn't need words. It felt too good to hold this man, and know he had awakened something inside her.

Something wonderful.

"You coming to the concert tonight?" he asked.

"Wouldn't miss it."

Chapter 12

If asked to select a soundtrack for her life, Jane would invariably choose silence. After ten steps onto the crowded main floor of the club her serene white light had been plundered. Aggression and sexual desire flooded her with invisible pokes to her psyche. The want and need bulging into every corner of the room swiftly assaulted her.

A strobe flittered manically from the edge of the stage, where a cavalcade of fans had taken to pounding on the shoulder-high stage. The entire room looked black, including floors, walls and ceilings, though it was actually a deep purple.

Remarkably, she made it to the balcony physically unscathed. Just when she thought a body would nudge into her, or out and out shove her, an arm or shoulder would merely skim her lightly. Sometimes the untouchable magic served a boon.

A knowing nod from a bouncer gestured her toward an empty table—the bands' table.

A table of over-makeuped, hair-sprayed women with Kleenex-sized shirts and artificial breasts giggled as Jane passed by and slid into the booth seat that formed a half curve and overlooked the dance floor and stage below.

"Jane?" A man in a gray suit with red pinstripes rushed over and offered a hand while sipping at what looked like a martini overflowing with olives. "Michael's girl?"

"Er, yes." Having it confirmed by a stranger made it more real. Yes, Michael's girl, and happy to be so, if not a little befuddled by the sensory assault.

"Phil Sloane," he offered. "The band's manager."

She shook his hand and had to shout as the announcer onstage let out a bellow to rouse the masses. "Is this where I'm supposed to be?"

The man made a hand motion from his eyes and toward the stage. "Right in Michael's eyesight. You got it! I'm working the room, but will return in a bit. What can I get you to drink?"

"White wine, please."

"No beer?" He smirked. "Where *did* Michael find you? I'll be right back!"

He hadn't exactly found her, she thought as she watched Phil sashay—yes, sashay—toward the upper-level bar. They had collided in a remarkable meeting of needs.

But whose need would get fulfilled? She could certainly help Michael. She'd been amazed to see the burns completely healed on his forehead and shoulder. All because of sex?

But what would *she* get out of it? Did she want something? Was she being selfish to consider that she should get equal satisfaction?

A drumbeat stirred the crowd to a roar. Jane winced. It took a while to adjust to the swell of noise, and before she could, three guitars joined the thumping drum.

Below, blind followers pumped their fists and bounced to the beat. Heads banged, hips rocked and the masses shouted to their musical heroes. A tremendous wave of aggressive energy billowed up from the dance floor.

It was fascinating to watch The Fallen perform live, though watching Michael was initially a bit disturbing. Unleashed mania and violent screams mastered the stage. Jane's head pounded with the resonance of Michael's plea to the masses. Gyrating and seething, he brewed The Fallen's lyrics into malicious incantations.

And his voice. Oh, but the man could slay angels with that controlled, yet manic yowl. He'd obviously studied, she guessed, for he could handle the double octave scales with ease and the drawn-out yowls—er, musical screams—were accomplished with a single breath.

Hadn't he said something about it all being about the scream?

The man mastered the room, commanding all to bear witness to his song. To succumb to his ministry of noise and erratic motion.

And sexy? Feline-like and frenetic, a long, lithe god on the stage, beating his head and swinging his hair, constantly moving and changing the air around him. He wore no shirt and the skin-tight black suede pants provided clear view of all that could be desired.

As the second song began, the three guitarists lined up along the edge of the stage and each ripped into their parts in head-banging synchronicity. Beating their heads to the rhythm, they played homage before their master—the crowd.

Michael drew up a wicked spell with his voice. Microphone his phallic totem, he spat out lyrics the entire audience sang along to. One arm thrust out before him, he conducted the crowd and gestured with his fingers towards himself, a symbol of wildness and exhilaration.

Releasing the corner of her lip she'd sucked in between her teeth, Jane smiled behind a swish of her hair.

And—she got it.

She now completely understood why women mooned over rock stars. Looking a warrior angel standing down the devil himself, Michael mastered the masses with his every move. A wild glimmer flashed in his eyes as he stretched his gaze across each and every banging head and cheering teenager. His smile gleamed brightly, catching the spotlight like sun on a blade.

And while the crowd ate it up, Michael tempted Jane up from the solace and tapped at the wall she'd so carefully built around her life. For decades she had been content to ignore the world, to simply exist. For to surrender to any one heart meant pain and suffering.

Wake up, sweet Jane.

What marvelous exhilaration contained within this vibrant, though troubled, man. She wanted Michael Lynsay, dark angel, singer extraordinaire. Vampire. She craved his energy and dark vitality.

For a glimmer, Jane latched gazes with Michael. Bobbing his head in time to the drumbeat, which set a slower pace for the next song, he winked at her. The crowd went wild. Everyone thought the wink for them.

But Jane knew differently. She could feel their connection across the room. And the shimmer, exclusive to the vampire, dove into her pores and inhabited her soul. He occupied her, stirring his wicked attraction into her innate magic. This is how it felt to live, to be alive.

Before he ripped into the lyrics, Michael whispered in the mike, "This is for sweet Jane."

The song wasn't a love song. Jane guessed the band didn't do sappy stuff like that. But when he sang a line about childhood memories and a walk in the garden, Michael again found her gaze.

"Oh, he's so perfect," cooed out from the table

next to Jane. "And he keeps looking up here! Did you see? I am so going to get into that man's pants tonight."

Jane laughed so hard she snorted.

"What's your problem?" The woman who mooned over Michael twisted and leaned over the black vinyl booth. "You think he was looking at you, sister?" She did a shoulder wiggle that moved her breasts in an amazing juggle. "He was looking at these double Ds, stick bitch. You got anything worth touching? I don't think so." She turned back to her girlfriends and they group high-fived each other.

The women were drunk. They were high-glossed floosies. Michael would never go for their sort.

Or would he?

Jane swept her gaze across the room, scanning the balcony and then down to the dance floor. Every female was tricked out in sexy clothing and makeup. There wasn't anything to choose from but these over-sexed plastic dolls. This was Michael's world. Of course these were his women.

Drawing up her leg and turning on the bench to look over the stage, she pressed a palm to her soft silk shirt. Size B cups underneath. No competition for the double Ds that had performed a lewd dance for her.

Oh, stop it; he doesn't care about breast size! And look at all that makeup. A man had to gag to kiss through all that thick red lipstick.

Maybe. A collection of underwear and bras?

"Jane Rénan?"

She turned to find someone had slid into the booth beside her. Jane stiffened. *Not Phil.* A young man with a crew cut and creepy blue eyes tugged at the zippered lapels of his jacket.

"How do you know my name? Are you with the crew?"

"I'm sorry, it's difficult to hear," he said as he leaned in, too close, and yelled into her ear. "I've something for you."

He reached inside his windbreaker and pulled out an iPod and laid it on the table before Jane.

"It belongs to your boyfriend," the guy said.

Michael had mentioned misplacing it in the graveyard.

"He is your boyfriend, yes?"

"Er, why do you ask?" She palmed the music player and slid it to the edge of the table. She wasn't about to give this kid information, especially if he was the photographer Michael had said he'd seen earlier. "What's your name?"

"It's Sylvan Banks." He offered his hand, but Jane didn't shake it. He shrugged, and retracted the friendly gesture. "Make sure your guy gets my name, will you? Can't say much more, but it'll all work itself out, soon enough. Nice to meet you, Ms. Rénan."

Too startled to reply, Jane merely watched as the kid slid out of the booth and insinuated himself into the crowd.

Well, that had been mysterious. She tapped the hard plastic shell of the music player. Had he looked through Michael's songs and other files? What things did Michael keep on here that might prove valuable to others?

Pulled back to the present by a spectacular drum crash, Jane glanced to the stage and met Michael's seeking gaze. She looked to the table next to her. A half dozen sets of breasts jiggled and flashed.

Jane had had enough.

Chapter 13

A gush of dry summer air and cigarette smoke crowded Michael's lungs. Two dozen women stood outside the back door to the club, most clutching scraps of paper in hopes of an autograph, which he ignored; instead he slapped a few hi-fives, and nodded at their effusive screams.

The glint of a gold cross flashed. An inexplicable cringe forced Michael to look away. *Avoid the holy.* He dodged to the right.

He didn't need The Fallen's logo T-shirt, so when some woman tore it off him, he let her. But he did like to wear pants. Thankfully, the bouncer charged out the back door and started wrangling women, two to an arm.

Michael was able to shimmy through the parking lot and stalk down the alleyway, away from the chaos, pants intact.

It was like walking away from his own party. The pull to return and bask in the adulation made him turn once and look back over the people loitering outside the club.

And he hadn't felt the urge to gnash his fangs and dig into anyone's neck. That was the positive about performing: a stage high was like the adrenaline rush of drinking blood. It would last him until morning. He was safe; the monster had been dragged around by a chain and put through the rounds. It wouldn't stir until tomorrow night.

But the ache now pounding in his chest felt different than the blood hunger. Something was missing, and he couldn't conceive of going home until he found it.

Michael rounded the corner and scanned the street fronted by half a dozen boutiques and bistros. There, out front of a bakery that touted *Fresh Croissants!* stood a copper-stained beauty talking to another he couldn't determine to be male or female.

"What the hell are you doing?" He crossed the street, arms spread and strides fast. "You can't leave without telling me."

The person talking to Jane turned to Michael. Hands at her hips and cocky stance screaming domination, she sniffed the air, and then snarled. "*This* is Michael?"

"Yes, Michael Lynsay, rock star with an

attitude," Jane said, sliding an "oh really?" look his direction. "Michael, this is Ravin Crosse, the woman I told you about."

"Ah." Blood draining to his toes, Michael took a mincing step back from the woman and put up placating hands. "I remember. The vigilante witch."

"He's a smart one. A rarity." Wearing leather vest and chaps, and obviously belonging to the chopper parked down the block, the woman commanded the atmosphere, despite her petite build. "I could do him right now and no one would be the wiser. Do you prefer a stake or blood bullet, vampire?"

"Ravin, I don't want Michael dead."

"Yeah," Michael started, but when Ravin turned her body toward Jane he saw the glint of moonlight on the huge silver cross around her neck. "Yeiahh! Woman, would you put that thing away?"

"Can't." She glanced a black-polished fingernail along the ornate silver. "Goes with the ensemble."

"Don't worry, Michael, I won't let her hurt you," Jane added.

He frowned at Jane.

"Listen, witch, cool your guns. I'm one of the good guys."

"There are no good vampires. The only good bloodsucker is a dead one." Ravin turned her attention to Jane. "This conversation isn't over, Jane. We've got to talk soon. Tomorrow." She sliced her gaze across Michael as she swept about. "Vampire."

The witch sauntered away, and on her back were two glinting pistols that Michael did not want to take a closer look at. She mounted the chopper, revved the engine, and took off.

"What's her deal?" he said after the bike had turned out of their view.

Jane sighed and announced lightly, "She doesn't like vampires."

"I caught that. Talk about uptight and looking for a fight."

"You know nothing about her. Ravin...she has issues."

"*Issues?* That dame has whole volumes."

"She's a friend."

"Yeah? What about me?"

"You are my man." She stretched her arms and yawned. The thin silk moved over her breasts but didn't conceal her hard nipples. Moonlight jealously slid across the lighter strands in her hair. "Show done?"

"Twenty minutes ago."

"I see you must have left at least one fan satisfied."

Michael stroked his bare chest, and felt the serrated flesh below his ribcage. The woman who'd torn off his shirt had used her nails. He hadn't noticed until now.

"Comes with the job. If I ever make it home with the same shirt I arrived in, well, something's wrong. Now, didn't I ask you to stay put?"

"I needed some fresh air. All the smoke and alcohol spattering me from every angle put disgust to a new level."

"Why didn't you tell someone where you were

going? Damn it, Jane! You can't go running off wherever you please."

"And why not? Because I'm Michael's girl and that implies some sort of ownership? You forgot to chain me to the table, lover, what did you expect?"

"Jane, what are you doing?"

"What are *you* doing? I'm perfectly capable of taking care of myself. I didn't wander far. And look, I ran into Ravin. If anyone could have protected me against a baddie, it would have been her."

"A baddie? Do you automatically consider vampires part of that group?"

"Michael, please."

"No, tell me. I've got to know if, when I'm making love to you, you're cringing inside. Or is that it? You're fulfilling some sort of fantasy every time you have sex with me?"

"I'm leaving. Obviously I'm not cut out to be your girl."

"Jane, don't be like that." Michael swept an arm around her back and pulled her close, nuzzling his nose into her hair. She didn't smell like lilacs, but smoke and booze and anger. "It was my fault."

No reply, but she did lift a brow.

"It was asking a lot," he said. "I should have waited and invited you to a smaller show." He shivered against her, her silk shirt tickling his bare chest. Yes, it was arousal, not the cool air, and oh yeah, those hard nipples begged for him to touch them. "But did you see? I was sending you love from the stage."

"Really?" She pulled back and stroked a finger along the tips of his sweat-saturated hair near his elbows. "Love, eh? Sounds pretty intense, especially since I'm only in it for my bad boy fix."

"You know what I mean. I care about you, Jane. I missed you during the last song. I wanted to sing only to you."

"Well, I'm sure the women next to the table where I had been sitting didn't mind you singing to them. They're double Ds, you know."

"Double—? Ha! Some fans are nuts. It's just part of the job."

"I think I'll hop in my car and head back to the house. You go on and party and do whatever it is you do after a gig. I'm sure it's all part of the job, right?"

"Jane."

"Michael, I'm tired. And I know I can't stand any more noise."

"You don't want me to come home with you?" He slid his hands from her back, gliding across the silk top, and around to caress her breasts. Impossible not to touch her. "I don't want to party with anyone but you and these size Bs."

Tilting her head down and smiling, she said, "How do you know what size they are?"

"I've had a some experience."

"I won't even ask."

She purred as he moved his thumbs up over her nipples, rocking the pads over the sweet insistent allure of her arousal. He nipped one of them through the silk. Since taking the stage, he had been riding an adrenaline high, but now, his world soared even further.

"Oh, Jane." Moving his lips along her neck, he teased at the vein, thick and pulsing with life. The tips of his canines were sharp weapons, but he did not will them down, nor did the lust draw them down without volition. He merely toyed with the idea of biting into her sweet smoke- and lilac-painted flesh. "This is too good."

Her fingernail skimmed his nipple. *Baby, touch me again. Right there. Don't be gentle.* He bit her neck, keeping his lips over his teeth so as not to break flesh.

"We shouldn't be doing this on the street in the middle of town," she murmured. "I want you, Michael." Her hand slid down the front of his pants. Her touch rocketed Michael's furious want to overdrive.

"No one's around," he reasoned. "We can move into the shadows beneath the awning of that store."

"Michael."

"Right. You drive. I'll do my best to distract you. Deal?"

"Come on, rock star. I drive well when distracted."

Jane stopped the Mini in the garage and shifted into Park. "You haven't kissed me for fifteen minutes. I'm feeling ignored."

"Let me unfold myself from this torture chamber, and then you had better watch out."

They poured out from the Mini, but didn't make it further than the bonnet of the car. Michael met Jane halfway, lifting her under the thighs and setting her on the tiny car hood. Bending into her, he rifled kisses along her neck and into her hair.

"You smell like smoke. But I think I found some flowers," he said. There, in the soft hollow at the base of her neck he smelled lilac. *Heady colored sex lure.* Shoving up the silk, he exposed her breasts and licked her hard nipples. "Did I tell you how much I enjoy lilacs?"

"A man who likes flowers? Pity they've completely spent their blooms."

"I could get into roses or whatever else you choose to tiptoe through barefoot." He growled when she wrapped her long legs about his hips and slammed his groin against hers. "You mean business, woman?"

"Of course I do. I'm the girl who got to take the lead singer home. You don't think I'll let him go without having my way with him, do you?"

"Oh, sweetness."

He slid a hand up under her skirt, conforming his fingers along the curve of her bottom. No panties. He was rock hard, and—and—no, he wasn't going to think about it. The monster hadn't shaken its chains.

"Let's go inside," she murmured. "The hood of the car is dirty."

"Baby, I don't think I'll make it that far."

Sharp fingernails dug into his chest. Michael

veered away, startled at her fire. She gave him a sneer, and leaped from the hood to dash inside.

He followed her inside and down the hall to the living room. Jane tugged a white canvas from the couch and tore it off to reveal beneath a lush green velvet sofa. Michael recognized it as some of Jesse's stuff from an apartment he'd had post high school.

"I thought you were tired?" he said as he made for the left side of the couch, but then did a fakeout and dashed to the right.

"You woke me up."

He jumped over the arm of the couch and gracefully lowered her to lie down. "You were never asleep, Jane, just hidden away. You've stepped out."

He slid up her shirt and tugged it over her head to toss to the floor. "I can't believe you let some bimbos upset you. Your breasts are gorgeous. And they taste like sin."

"What does sin taste like?" She directed his head to pay full respect to both breasts, and Michael followed her lead.

"Like smoke and flowers. Now let's get this skirt off you. Ooooh, yes."

She'd found something that interested her. Yes, right there. Michael groaned. Almighty demons, the woman was not meek. Her fingers cupped his crotch, exploring the shape of his hard-on through the suede pants.

"You first," she purred. "I think these pants are too tight, and mighty uncomfortable."

She'd already tugged the leather laces free, so Michael had only to shrug the pants from his hips,

Jane slid to the floor before him. Knees parted to either side of his feet, she looked up at him. No angel had ever smiled so wickedly.

First kiss of her lips to his *attitude* and the world literally rocked.

Tossing back his head and pushing his fingers through Jane's copper tousle, Michael closed his eyes to the sinful touch of this devil's daughter.

Sweet Jane of the garden flowers and bare feet. He knew this woman had lived more lifetimes than he could ever imagine. She had experienced the world, and had likely many lovers to perfect her prowess. Jane was no wilted flower who shied from her own passions.

"Oh, baby." He tensed his jaw and prepared for the release. "Yeess."

He could not wait, and he would not. Michael came with a twist of bittersweet darkness. She took his climax into her mouth—but he couldn't lift her up to kiss her, to nuzzle into her hair and then slip a finger into her to coax her to orgasm.

His fangs had come out to play. The monster had snuck up on him without warning. He hadn't sensed the hunger.

Now it was too late.

He shoved her hard onto the couch. "Get out! I don't want to hurt you!"

Crouched on the couch, Jane wiped her mouth with a swipe of her hand. She wore him on her lips.

Even as she scrambled over the back of the couch, Michael lunged and caught the hem of her skirt. Jane tumbled to the floor and hit the hardwood with a cry of pain.

Grabbing his pants and slipping them back up around his hips, Michael shouted again for her to hurry, as Jane managed to pull herself up. She didn't even look at him. Her pink skirts breezed out of the room. Bare feet scampered up the stairs.

The vampire lunged around the couch, and as he passed through the door, his body jerked and convulsed. Catching his palms against the doorjamb, Michael coiled down and into himself. So strong, this urge. It clawed. It growled. The body had gotten satisfaction.

Now it was time for the real hunger.

"Why can't I stop this?" He winced so hard his entire face grew hot and he felt sure a vein would burst and pour out the tainted blood that flowed through him. "I've got to fight it."

Go get her.

Running the hallway, his feet took action before his brain could decide if it was right or wrong. It wasn't right. He'd made Jane a promise he would not harm her.

It does them no harm! The blood extraction brings them great pleasure. Give it to her!

"Jane!"

Chapter 14

Jane felt sure no bolt lock the size of her littlest finger would keep anything out from her room tonight. Not a raging rock star. Not a furious monster.

Eyeing the corner of the bed frame, she struggled with a flashing thought. The frame was wood, the post topped by a fist-sized whitewashed ball. She could twist off the leg and smash it in half. A stake.

"No. Can't do that to him," she murmured. "What else?"

Her entire fortune for a cross or splash of holy water right now. It wouldn't serve any more than give him a nasty burn, and maybe quiet the raging beast for the night. Long enough to get him to the coffin, where the darkness would settle his soul and he'd succumb to sleep. And she'd been thinking the coffin ridiculous.

While she knew her own blood might serve the ultimate weapon against a vampire, she had not once taken life, and didn't intend to start anytime soon— or until the full moon arrived.

Rushing into the bathroom, she pulled open the medicine cabinet. Out in the bedroom, the door rattled on the hinges. Michael growled. The beast wanted blood.

The beast could break down the door if it wanted to, so some moral code deep within Michael held him at bay.

All she had was a toothbrush, toothpaste, a plastic razor and…a bottle of aspirin. Two hundred and fifty count aspirin.

"Should keep him busy for a while."

Gripping the bottle, she tore off the cover and pried away the tight silver seal. She'd have to be spare with them.

Scratches and kicks punctuated the vampire's angry hunger.

There was no way Michael could rise above the innate need to feed. He'd slipped into a wicked routine of sex, blood and rock 'n' roll. Had she been a fool to believe that anything could change him?

The wood door creaked and a thick bolt flew through the air, missing Jane's cheek by spare inches.

And there he stood, chest bared and heaving,

arms curved out at his sides. One of the fallen fighting his way up from hell. A man struggling to control his dark impulses.

"Run, Jane," he hissed. "Please."

"No." She never ran away from a challenge. Besides, there was nowhere to run.

"We had a deal. You run when I tell you to. Don't make me regret my actions."

"Just breathe, Michael. Take deep breaths and try to calm yourself."

"Too late." He licked his lower lip. "I can't get the scent of your blood from my nose. You're inside me, Jane."

He stepped into the room, his pace stiff, awkward. He tried to fight the monster, to hold it back. She felt it.

"I've got…" She held up the plastic bottle. "Oh *mon Dieu.* I hope this works."

Scattering half the contents on the floor, she then stepped back and around to the other side of the bed, putting a barrier between she and Michael. He stepped over the mess, but paused on the other side and looked down at the tiny white pills.

"What the hell?"

"Aren't they pretty?" Jane said as she climbed over the bed and made her way cautiously out of his peripheral vision. "You should count them."

"Count—are you freakin'—?" Arms curled and chest huffing, Michael snapped backwards to look over his shoulder. "Although…"

Cocking his head, a curious beast, the man stared

at the floor. No longer did he huff and growl. His entire body bent to study the aspirins.

"There must be hundreds. Why did you spill them? Jane. Where are you going? We're not finished. I'm coming after you. One, two, three…"

Reaching the door, which hung from one bolt, Jane dropped another aspirin on the floor. Michael saw, but he spread his fingers over the pills before him, unwilling to leave his treasure.

"That's right, Michael. I've got more." Backing down the hallway and toward the stairs, she dropped aspirins in a trail. Leading the creature to his lair. She prayed this would not backfire on her.

Crouched intently, he appeared in the doorway, picking up the aspirins and whispering his tally as he followed her down the hall and the stairs.

When she reached the bottom of the basement stairs, Jane dumped the last few aspirins into the open coffin and stepped into the shadows. Sliding along the wall as Michael descended into the darkness, she stretched out and slapped his clutched fist.

Aspirins flew everywhere, landing on the cement floor and skittering into the shadows.

"What did you do that for?" He lunged for her. Jane dodged but tripped, landing the on bottom step. Michael's hot breath hissed at her ear. "I've got you now. You smell so…oh…damn you, but you're mine."

"Take me then, vampire." Smoke and tangible anger curdled her desire. But his closeness ever drew her into his exotic allure. He could have her… "Oh! Did you get that one?"

"Huh?" He looked to the aspirin she pointed to. The vampire twisted a kink from his neck and bent to count. "One." He spied the next pill and crept over to it. "Two."

Relieved to have escaped her own shortcomings, Jane scrambled up the stairs. "This is for your own good, Michael. Please, stay down here. Try to sleep it off."

She slammed the door at the top of the stairs. It didn't have a bolt, not even a simple push-button lock in the knob.

Blowing strands of hair from her face, Jane settled against the wall. There was no sense in running. He either took her advice, and slept it off, or the monster would soon be knocking at her door. This was going to be a long night.

The beast slept. In fact, Jane didn't hear stirring below until well into afternoon the following day. Though angry at him for raging at her last night, she couldn't make herself hate him for it.

The train had gone off the tracks. When she had started to care about him? After their first kiss in the garden?

No, it had been the morning after they'd first made love and she'd woken up amidst a bed of roses. And she'd looked for the burn on his face and had found none. Healed.

So no, she would not fault him for slipping last

night. The man was an addict. Addictions were not cured, they were managed. And they had slowly begun to manage the monster inside Michael.

As Jane put the finishing touches to window number three, she heard the floorboards out in the hallway creak. Not turning to acknowledge him, because she wanted to keep a finger to the last seam so it sealed properly, Jane listened as Michael padded around behind her.

Pacing? The scruff of his suede pants sounded ridiculously loud. Ever in motion. Alive with chaotic sensuality. Impossible to pick up on his breathing, so she couldn't determine his mood. Yet her magic lifted, seeking to put up a barrier. Had it been her inner charm that ultimately kept the vampire at bay last night?

The source. Come on, Jane, this man was dropped into your lap. You don't need Ravin. What you need is to stop this idiot caring business.

Closing her eyes tightly, Jane fought against the nasty little devil on her shoulder.

He would have bitten you. Why shouldn't you use him?

Finally Michael walked around the opposite side of the plywood table and studied her work for a few moments. Not having the words to speak that would make her feel any different about last night, or him, she decided silence was best.

He inhaled and leaned over the plywood. A fist pounded the wood, upsetting her glass pieces. Spreading out his hand, dozens of tiny white pills spilled across a cut portion of vibrant scarlet glass.

His mouth moved into a quick curve. "What," he said, "in all the world was this for?"

Heartened by his smile, Jane released her breath. For a moment there she wouldn't have been surprised to have him lunge for her and finish what he had tried to start last night.

She shook her head, marveling at the power she had wielded in utilizing such an average item. Yes, aspirins.

"The best way to defeat a vampire?" she said. "Give them something to count. Myth and lore tells how peasants used to bury prospective vampires with fishing nets. If the dead body revived to go out and seek blood, it couldn't because it would have to count the knots in the net first. Didn't you know that?"

"During moments like last night, I don't know much beyond the blood hunger. I want. I feed. So…give me something to count, and I'm defeated?"

"It worked, didn't it?"

He toggled an aspirin and chuckled, then he stepped back and let loose a burst of laughter. "Oh, Jane. You tamed the vicious vampire last night. You and your bottle of pills."

Suddenly Michael smacked his forehead with an open palm. "Jane, I've had an epiphany. I can't believe it. All this time…" He ran his fingers back through his hair. "I've always been a counter. Isn't that freaky?"

"Makes sense."

"Doesn't it?"

"So," she released hold on the seam, "you're feeling less peckish today?"

"Yes. I managed to get myself in order once down in the dark. Alone with my aspirins. So, like anything? A bunch of stones or a pile of guitar picks? Anything to count?"

She nodded.

"That's so bizarre."

"Much safer than a stake, wouldn't you say?"

He jerked his attention across the table. A spot of something close to fear glittered in each eye. "You wouldn't?"

"I considered it." He deserved to know how desperate she had been. It wasn't every day a girl goes from nine on a sexual pleasure scale and is jerked down to a negative one within a snap.

"Seriously?"

"Seriously." She brushed remnants of copper tape from the window and stood back to look over her work.

"That's harsh, Jane. I would never harm you, I've told you that."

"And I believe you. But it wasn't you who broke down my bedroom door last night, was it?"

"If I said it was the darkness inside of me, it would be an excuse. I've got to lay claim to the monster. It's as much a part of me as my breath."

"That's the smartest thing I've heard you say since we've met."

No, she couldn't walk away from the vampire. Nor would she consider him for the ritual. That wasn't going to happen. There were some things in life not worth a sacrifice. Like this man's trust.

"I think we went a little too far last night. We should have taken things more slowly."

"Too far? Jane, I don't know where you learned to make love like that, but there was no slowing down once you started."

"Exactly. Michael, I'm serious. I mean, we've got to slow the sex down."

"Slow is good." He leaned across the plywood table and his hair brushed over her hand. "All night long, the two of us, wrapped in each other's arms."

"Yes, well, that's why I think it worked when we were in the shower. We were both tired, taking things slowly. And maybe your senses were distracted by the water. You couldn't focus on the angry need inside you."

"Possibly."

"Probably. We've got to be reasonable about this. It's either slow out of the gate or else take precautions."

"What does that mean? Can you get pregnant? Of course you can." He swiped a palm over his mouth, shaking his head. "I'm sorry, I wasn't thinking."

"I *can* get pregnant. After all, my mother and father had me. But don't worry, it's not the right time of the month."

"The right time? Are you on birth control?"

"No, but I know my cycle. But you should pick up some condoms next time you're in town."

"Will do."

Moving a few pieces of emerald glass together, Jane formed what would be a leaf set into the lower quadrant of window number three. Michael collected the aspirins and tossed them into the box she kept under the table for scraps.

"So," she asked, "how do you feel today?"

"Good."

"Better?"

"You mean, stronger? More powerful? Yes, I think so. And we didn't even complete the sex last night. It's really working, Jane."

"Glad to know I can help."

"I'm not doing this just to gain power, Jane. If you think that…"

"I don't. I know it's something else entirely."

"It is. Or is it? Is it your magic that draws me? Are you making me do this?"

She dropped a piece of glass and it snapped in two. "How dare you even suggest that. Michael, I do not need to influence any man to have sex with me. Damn it!" She tossed the broken pieces in the box and stomped away from him toward the windows.

Stupid man. So self-possessed.

She stomped her foot again, feeling the need to plunge into her anger.

Michael saw the window teeter, but even as he opened his mouth to warn Jane, he knew it would be too late. He rushed across the room as the eight-foot tall window silently tilted forward.

Jane swung about, sighting the movement, and cringed.

"No, run!" he hissed, but it was too late.

The window fell. Exquisite myriad colors sailed through the air, heading toward the artist. He waited for Jane's scream. But it did not come.

Nor did the window crash and break into a million glittering splinters.

Jane stood in a crouch, her hands put up to block the window. Glass fit together in colored sections of azure and crimson and emerald hovered but inches from her fingers. The entire window hung suspended, mid fall—unbroken.

"Bloody hell. She's...holding it back?"

Michael wasn't sure what to do. He could whisk her away from a sure and ugly death. He could grab the window and toss it aside. Which would prove a faster move?

Before he could decide, the glass cracked and continued its fall to the floor.

Jane still did not scream. She didn't even move. And while she faced the falling glass, her mouth open in horror, not a single shard sliced her body.

Ruby glass sparkled and crashed into the hardwood. Azure slivers, glinting along the deadly edges, scattered and sprayed everywhere. Every color broke away, and slid around Jane, to die a vivid death at her feet.

And when it was all over, Michael grabbed Jane and whisked her out from the fallen shards. She clung to him, shaking. Fear scent loomed about her like a swarm of insects thick in her hair.

Michael gripped her tightly, wanting to press her

into him, if only to be safe. And yet, the aroma of her fear drew down his teeth. He stretched out his mouth, fighting back the involuntary need.

"Michael?"

His entire body rigid to fight the want, he hugged her tighter, granting comfort while fighting himself.

There on the floor, in the exact outline of where Jane had stood, lay no glass.

"It fell around you?"

Jane turned within Michael's tight hold to look over the disaster. She reached back, clutching at his suede pants, finding his hips and digging in her fingernails. He moaned.

"Mon Dieu," she murmured. "It's really working."

A shiver of fear moved her body against his—no, no more fear. Michael no longer felt the acrid tinge of anxiety sweeping into his pores, instead, it had been replaced with that fruity cheery feeling he'd initially felt upon meeting this woman. Elation overtook Jane's fear—and his teeth retracted.

"Whew."

"What?" She looked to him, but remained completely unaware of what he'd just struggled with.

"I don't understand," he said. "Why didn't the glass tear through you? Jane?"

"That would have never happened weeks earlier," she said. "It happened so fast, but...I *willed* it to avoid me. I invoked my magic, Michael. *I* did that."

"How? You mean...from me?"

She nodded and moved to investigate, but he pulled her back to him. She was barefoot. "Let me carry you out of here, and then I'll sweep it up." He lifted her into his arms and she embraced and kissed him. "From me? Really?"

"I wasn't sure if it would happen, so I didn't say anything. When we make love, you draw out my magic. But you also draw it up, making it accessible to me. For some reason, Michael, you've unleashed the magic I've not been able to control since birth."

"So—" if he understood this correctly "—we're good for each other?"

"Yes."

"Huh." He strode out from the workroom, avoiding the glass, and didn't set Jane down until he'd reached the kitchen. "I'm not sure how I feel about this."

"What do you mean?" She grabbed the champagne and crème de cassis from the fridge. "Wait." The bottles clunked onto the table, echoing her sudden switch in moods. "You have no problem taking from me, but now that you've learned I'm taking from you as well—?"

"I admit it. It's just…not right."

"How typical of a man." She marched away from him, heading out the back door.

And Michael remained, fending off the shudder he felt from the invisible slap Jane had sent his way. He'd felt it. Had it been her magic, or was it something he imagined after feeling her cold remark?

"This is not good."

There was no way he was going to allow any woman the upper hand.

Chapter 15

The next morning, Jane joined Ravin at a table in the back of a Panera restaurant. Ravin had already taken the liberty of ordering Jane a slice of pie. It was still steaming when she sat down, though Ravin's French Silk pie had been reduced to mere crust and a few traces of whipped cream.

"Good to see you again," Jane said as she sipped the fresh coffee the waitress dropped off for her.

"Drop the small talk, Jane. I just saw you last night. With a vampire."

"Very perceptive. Oh, that's right, you have the Sight."

"Don't play with me. We've been friends too long."

The waitress stopped to top off Jane's ice water.

Ravin stretched an arm across the padded bench and tilted a seriously discerning gaze over Jane. "You know, now that we're sitting here in the daylight, you look good. Much better than you did a week ago. Really good, actually. The country must agree with you, eh? If I didn't know better, I'd say you look I've-been-having-incredible-sex good, but I know you wouldn't have sex with a vampire."

Jane lifted a smug smile to her friend. "And how do you know that?"

"Oh, Jane, don't tell me you've been letting that bloodsucker jump you?"

"You make it sound as if I'm a meek woman, who cowers and lets any man do as he wishes with me."

Ravin sniffed and splayed out her hands. "Does he?" She wore the usual leathers today. Biker gear, Jane supposed. Imposing, is what it was.

"I probably wanted him before he wanted me."

No reply, just that all-knowing, judgmental eyebrow lift. It held centuries of pain in that simple move, but Jane wasn't about to let it get to her. Ravin sighed heavily and nodded to the table. "You going to eat your pie?"

Jane blew on the steam. She liked hot pie. "Soon. Go ahead, order another slice."

Ravin flagged the waitress and got another slice. Two bites obliterated half the slim slice and Ravin showed no signs of slowing down. "So, we've both tagged the same source, which is now a very unusable source thanks to his public persona."

"I wouldn't use Michael even if he wasn't famous."

Ravin stabbed her pie with the fork. A twist mangled the innards. "Jane, you're in too deep. This is not acceptable. He's using you for your magic, there's no other explanation."

"And what if I'm using him?" Jane lifted her own challenging eyebrow at her friend. "He's the reason I'm so glowy."

"No." Ravin put up a splayed hand. "Don't even go there, Jane. I don't want to hear this."

"Ravin."

"Jane."

Jane leaned across the table, scanned the nearby diners and found none interested in their conversation, and then lowered her voice. "It was purely accidental. Neither of us knew about the other, and then when we were already going at it—"

"I said I don't want details. Mother of— Bloody hell, are you insane? You are sleeping with a nasty longtooth? A bloodsucker!"

"My mother does it every night."

"That's different!" Ravin shoved her empty plate and it clanked against Jane's water glass.

The women checked their periphery. A few diners glanced their way, then guiltily returned to their breakfast plates.

In quieter tones, Ravin hissed, "He's using you."

"Is not."

"Why else would a vampire risk sleeping with the enemy? He's getting something from you, Jane. Your magic! Don't you know they can suck it right out from you every time you have sex? They don't even have to bite, it flows into them somehow. During sex. I don't even want to think of how it happens."

"I do know that, and I've seen it work. Michael was burned by the sun, and sex healed him."

"Oh, hell." Ravin was silent for a moment, gathering steam. "And you don't find anything at all wrong with that? Of course not! Because you can't resist. He's enslaving you, Jane."

"Ridiculous. I can stop any time I want."

"But he can't. You've become his supplicant. The more sex he gets from you, the more magic he takes, and the more magic he gains, the more his body craves it. Don't you see? Your magic is like a drug to him. And the only result will be one hell of a powerful vampire, and you will be his idiot slave."

"I'm getting something from him, too!"

"Oh?" Ravin sat back and lifted her fork. She'd lost interest in food, instead stabbing the wedge of crust with the tines. "What? Are you waiting for the right time, then *wham,* make him bite you and he's ash? That's a good plan, you know. I've lured a few vamps to their death by offering up my neck. But never sex, Jane. You don't do vampires. Got it?"

"I'm not like you, Ravin. I don't hate vampires. My father is one!"

"Right. Well, then. Go ahead, ransom your freedom to a bloody longtooth. Let him have his way with you. Let's hope he sticks around long enough for the ritual—"

"I would never dream to use Michael for the ritual."

Ravin tilted a brow and the sigh that followed needed no interpretation. "You're in trouble, Jane. I think I need to pay you a visit and put some fear into that vampire. If not a stake."

"Absolutely not. I know what I'm doing." She sat back and stared at her pie, and then realized something odd, but actually very wonderful. "See?" She pointed to the steaming slice of apple pie. "It's still hot."

"So?"

"We've been here for half an hour. It should be cold by now. Don't you understand, Ravin? I think Michael is drawing up *my* magic. The stuff I've never been able to tap into my entire life. I've even controlled it right now. I wanted a hot slice, and look."

"That's…not right. But maybe. I don't know why that should work, but— It's probably just wishcraft."

"An integral part of a witch's magic. Don't rule it out, Ravin. If having sex with Michael will draw up my magic to a point where I can begin to use and control it, well, that would be amazing."

"And in the meantime you're creating a superpowerful vampire who, while he may be increasing your magic, is draining as much from you for his own use."

"It's not like he can become one of the bewitched. He'd need to drink my blood for that."

"*Is* that impossible?"

Jane shrugged. "I don't know, but I'm not going to take the chance on Michael."

"What if I found two sources for you? One for the ritual, the other, to snack on your blood? That way, you'd know for sure."

"You'd help me so I can know for sure whether or not Michael can take my blood?"

Ravin slumped back on the bench. "You're right. Stupid idea. I don't know what I was thinking. You know I actually don't care now if he is a public figure. If I see him again, Jane, I'm staking the bastard."

"You do, and we are no longer friends."

Ravin drew up tall on the bench, her eyes leveling with Jane's. Dark and without a glint, that was the stare she likely used to face down the enemy before obliterating them.

But Jane was serious, too. She would suffer no witch should she harm Michael.

"He's already begun to enslave you," Ravin said. "You just can't see it. You think it's love, but it's subservience. I'm not going to let that happen to a good friend."

"A good friend who sees vampires in a very different light than you, remember that, Ravin."

Struck by the truth, Ravin settled her defensive posture and dropped her shoulders.

"How is your father these days? What would he think if he knew his daughter was doing a vamp?"

"I haven't spoken to him for months. And he wouldn't care."

"Oh, no? I don't know Baptiste Rénan personally, but from what you've told me, he wouldn't be too keen on his daughter's enslavement."

"I am *not*—" Jane checked her voice and lowered it "—a slave. I'm taking as much as he is getting." She shoved her plate to the center of the table and began to rifle through her purse for change. "I'm not hungry anymore. I should be getting back."

"Because you're *compelled* to return to him?"

"Ravin, please trust that I can take care of myself."

"And what about that source you need in *less than a week?* Can you take care of that yourself?"

"No. For that, I still need your help. I wouldn't know where to begin the search for another vampire."

"You could start by looking between your sheets."

"Please, Ravin?"

The petite powerhouse swung out of the booth. She tossed a twenty-dollar bill on the table, and shoved her hands into her back pockets.

"I hope you know what you're doing, Jane. But in case you don't, I've got your back." With that, she turned and marched out.

And Jane, sighing into the steam rising from her pie, wondered if maybe she was falling a little too quickly for Michael.

She sat on the couch before the imposing field-stone hearth that smelled like winter fires and promised cozy warmth. The couch and a chair were the only furniture in the room, and both were covered over with thick white canvas. Michael imagined the dust must have flown when she'd first sat down, for he could smell the musty dryness and feel the motes creep down his throat.

He smiled again. Entering Jane's aura was all it took. It was her magic, he knew that now, because he'd become attuned to that certain tingle. It lived inside him, thanks to making love to her.

In a well-executed move he gripped the back of the couch and leaped to sit next to Jane. He landed close, so that their shoulders connected, and he felt the tug of her skirt as she shifted her leg to free her foot from beneath his thigh.

"What's up?" he asked. "You're not working?"

"Taking a break. Thinking."

She placed her palm on his thigh. Not a sexual touch, more like she was concentrating, trying to test for, well, he didn't know. For a long while she held there, then suddenly jerked her hand away.

"The shimmer," she whispered, and smiled a little. "Tell me about yourself, Michael. How long have you been a vampire?"

He stared at the side of her face. Impossibly smooth skin. Soft, delicious mouth that tasted better than cherries. Tilting her head with a touch, he kissed the corner of her mouth. She didn't react, but he didn't need her to reciprocate. He liked to explore her. It was easier to control his needs when around her now. He knew it was because of the sex magic.

"I was changed in the sixties. I've been a vamp

for almost fifty years. Not long in the greater scheme of things, I know."

He stretched out a leg, crossing it over hers, imposing himself on her careful containment. "My blood master was a cruel bitch."

"A woman?"

"Yes, a woman. First she seduced me, then, when she grew tired of me, she decided to reveal her vampire nature, and proceeded to transform me. And then she left. That very same night."

"Seriously?"

"Yes. I believe it went something like—Michael, I love you. *Chomp.* See ya later, big boy. Just like that. No card, no letters. I haven't seen her since."

"Do you regret it?"

"What I am? Not at all. I am what I am, and I'm a damn good vampire. Not many could take the stage like I do and still keep the secret. But I do regret the manner in which it was done. It all happened so fast. I had no time to take it in, and then she was gone."

"You were in love with her?"

A vision of Isabelle LaPierre walked before Michael's memory. Everything about her so pale, so utterly delicate and priceless. He'd followed her home that first night he'd seen her alone at the movie theater. It had been a thriller about a thief who had stolen a jewel. Isabelle had stolen his heart.

"Of course I was in love with her. We were together six months before she revealed she was a vampire. I had absolutely no clue, can you believe that?"

"She must have fed before she was with you."

Jane's droll recital of things she *thought* she knew wasn't necessary. She couldn't know his past. That was for him to own.

"Do you still pine for her?"

"No." Spoken quickly. Because, well—no, he didn't pine. But he did often wonder. "She is my past now. I'm not sure she even lives. And since, I've never had a girlfriend. Life is much easier without commitment."

"And when you struggle with the blood sex thing so much."

"Yes. There are days I don't think I could have a relationship if I tried. And yet…" He clasped her hand and brought it to his lips to press. "Look what we're doing. I've had sex without biting. That's nothing less than amazing, Jane."

He leaned in and cupped her head, pressing his nose to her cheek. "I want more of you. I want you now, I want you later, I want you all day, everyday, surrounding me and cleaving to me."

"Do you—" he felt a tremble in her arm as she slid it from his grasp and along her thigh "—want to enslave me?"

"No." He closed his eyes and kissed her hard. Where had that come from?

Did he want to enslave her? Was it possible to do so without knowing it? He knew that he was drawn to her magic again and again, like a drug. Like adrenaline. Sex magic had been effective in steering him from that addiction.

"Maybe. I don't want you to be subservient to me, Jane. I would never want that. But, I do want you to be mine."

"At the risk of your death?"

"Yes, even at such a risk. So long as we're agreed on the plan. I say run, you do so. I think we can make this work."

"I don't want to run for ever, Michael. I want you to control the hunger. I think you can."

"Impossible to promise it can be that way every time. Sex without blood…isn't right."

"So the sex we've had hasn't been right?"

"It's been great. Just…" He sighed. There *was* something missing. But when weighing the option of orgasm to death, there wasn't much of a choice, was there?

Sucking in air, Michael struggled with the situation. To have another know about his dark addiction, and to be so casual about it, felt surreal. Like the spotlight had been shifted from outside of him, to inside, deep in his chest where he once felt the loneliest.

When he'd stood on stage the other night, for the first time, he had not felt alone. For he knew Jane was there, in the shadows, and in his heartbeats.

"I've already explained I need a blood exchange to bond with you completely. But I know that can never be, so I accept that."

"Really?" She snuggled against him.

Michael stroked her hair. "Really."

But it was a lie. He wanted more from Jane.

Because even though she was a part of him, racing through his veins on a steady beat, they would always be a background harmony. Never a melody.

Isabelle's pulse was still a part of him. He had merely to think of her and that slow, sultry movement glided through his veins. He hadn't thought of her for a long time. And the only way to be completely rid of her was to replace her blood pulse with another's.

"Didn't you say that it was your birthday soon?"

"Yes." He stirred from the rhythm of Isabelle's memory. "A few days."

"Do you want to celebrate?"

"Sure. You like parties?"

"Do you?"

"I can do a private one. Just the two of us. A little wine, some dancing, music."

"The radio reception out here sucks, and with my iPod gone, I'm afraid we're out of luck."

"Oh, I almost forgot!" Jane stood and rushed out to the garage. "I know I stuck it in my pocket the night of the concert. I think it must have slipped out on the drive home."

She opened the door to the Mini and started sorting about. "Here it is!" She turned to present Michael with the iPod.

"Where'd you find this? Was it in the car the whole time?"

"No." She closed the door and leaned against it, crossing her arms under her breasts. "Some kid gave it to me last night at the club. He said he found it, and I assumed it was the reporter from the graveyard. Sylvan Banks, that was the name he gave me. He said something cryptic like 'Michael will know the truth soon enough.'"

"Bastard." Michael flicked on the music player and filed through the various programs. "I suppose he looked through my address book and at the unreleased songs." He thumbed over the Video selection, thinking to check the play count.

A face flashed onto the small screen. Briefly, but in that two seconds the image burned itself onto the screen.

"Cripes!" Michael dropped the iPod and, faltering, caught himself against the iron railing fronting the stairs.

"What is it? Michael?"

He bent and leaned over the iPod. The screen faced him, but instead of a colored video stream a small file folder flashed at him. He must have screwed it up when dropping it.

But that face. He knew that face.

"Did he do something to your stuff? Michael?" Jane tapped his arm. "Talk to me."

"I think I just saw a ghost."

Chapter 16

He had picked her lily of the valley on Monday. On Tuesday, he picked her yellow tulips he discovered out back beneath a loose pile of dried leaves. Wednesday, he'd called into town to have roses delivered because he'd picked all the new growth from the garden.

On Thursday, Michael unwrapped four dozen peonies with heads as big as a baby's. Streaks of white painted the deep crimson inner petals. They smelled like exotic wine. The North Lake floral shop loved him.

Jane had asked Michael to meet her in the basement this evening—she had a surprise for him— so he wrapped his arms around the unwieldy bouquet and, blossoms bouncing like a drummer's head, went in search of a lady in need of wooing and many, many flowers.

The entire house smelled like a garden. He'd even allowed her to place a vase of daisies in the recording studio; though, those didn't smell great.

Jane invaded his soul like a creeping vine spilling over with ruffle-petaled flowers. And he didn't mind it one bit. In fact, it kept his mind from his reality.

Because really, this wasn't reality, this sharing a home with Jane, was it? No, it was more a fantasy he'd never hoped to live. She wasn't his type of woman. He wasn't her kind of man. She'd made it very clear there would never be a blood bond between them. There could not be two more opposite beings. Hell, they were natural enemies. Never, would they have the sort of connection he craved.

Yet he didn't want the fantasy to end.

Cruising by the studio he glanced inside. Michael stopped, his focus fixing to the iPod. It had been a ghost, or some kind of look-alike. Couldn't be anything but. But how had the image of that woman gotten onto his iPod? Had the reporter put it on there? He had to.

That didn't explain a thing. How would the reporter know about anything that could upset Michael?

Nah, it was probably just a clip from one of his files, a flash from an old video that featured a remarkable face that simply reminded him of his past. To really know, he needed to access the files, but after dropping it, the thing now pleaded to be reformatted and the original software was at home in Los Angeles.

He vacillated between having it sent so he could reboot the file and check it again, or just convincing himself he'd seen nothing more than a fragment of a file with a familiar face.

Unwilling to believe in a prank, Michael decided it was a coincidence. He'd been thinking about her and, with her image still fresh in mind, he'd imagined it on the iPod.

Michael shuffled down the basement steps and into the lit room. "Jane? Where'd you find the lamp?"

"It's from my studio. Oh, those are gorgeous."

She plunged into his arms, and between them, the crushed flowers wept a heady perfume.

"I love peonies even more than roses." She dipped her head into the flowers and closed her eyes to draw in the scent. "They're like wine, don't you think? Intoxicating."

"Nothing could be more addictive than you— what the hell?"

Now Michael noticed the chains dangling from the far wall. They hadn't been there yesterday. Huge black manacles hung at the end of each chain. They were spaced about six feet apart, and secured to the concrete wall by an iron plate and four huge bolts.

"You like?"

"I—what?" The flowers fell from his arms and, though Jane caught some, he trampled the peony blossoms with his boots as he crossed the room. "Is this your surprise?" He tapped one of the manacles. "Please tell me this is not my surprise."

"This is your surprise." She bopped him on the shoulder with a flower. "So take off your clothes."

Michael spun around so quickly he lost his balance. Either that or she'd put a spell on him to make him woozy and surrender to her wicked commands. Could be the inner magic she possessed. Which was no longer as *inner* as it had once been.

"You're serious?"

"I'm always serious."

"You're not going to do magical experiments on me?"

"Now that *is* an idea. But no, Michael, I want to have sex. Don't you?"

"Stupid question, Jane."

"I figured so. But, much as I know we both want it, we need to keep the beast in chains."

Michael scratched his head. "No way. It's impossible." At least, that was his initial reaction… But. He scruffed fingers back through his hair. "Really?"

He vacillated between dread and a weird sexual fascination. The woman actually suggested he let her chain him to the wall and allow her to have her way with him.

Hands sliding into his pockets, he leaned forward to inspect the manacles. "Where's the key?"

"Upstairs, with the instructions. I haven't had time to read through them."

"They come with instructions? Jane," he breathed. "You are so not serious."

"Yes, instructions. And I was surprised because I didn't order them from some kinky sex shop. I didn't think they'd be strong enough, so I called an industrial supplier I've used for my work. I had the deliveryman install them this morning while you were sequestered in the studio. So," blithely unaware of his reluctance, she commanded, "strip."

"Sure." Michael stared at the chains. Cold, hard and black, they looked like something a death metal band would use for a prop. Call him outrageous and uninhibited on stage, but at home in bed he liked things simple and unimposing.

Maybe.

He'd never tried the kinky stuff so he shouldn't rule it out.

"Michael." Her hands slid down his chest, and she dug her nails in the wake.

Working the buttons slowly, Michael eventually slid off his long-sleeve shirt—a favorite that sported red skulls against black—and let it drop to the floor. "So what has it been, a couple weeks we've known each other? Suddenly Jezebel reveals herself?"

Jane propped a hand on her hip. "Got a problem with that?"

"There are too many ways to go with this one, sweetie. I think I'll defer to you and your worldly wisdom. Wait. Have you done this with previous lovers?"

"Michael."

"I need to know."

"Never. Cross my heart."

"No, don't—cross anything. Please."

"Sorry. I should know better, having avoided it around my father. So. Strip."

"I'm working on it. But I do think we're going to need a safe word or something."

"Stained glass," she said over his shoulder, because he'd yet to tear his gaze from the black chains. "That's the word, er, words. You say them, I'll back off. Promise."

Jeans unzipped, but still at his hips, Michael turned to Jane. Floaty strands of hair listed across her face. Her pale smile taunted him so wickedly. "Just what are your intentions, young lady? You got some whips hidden in the coffin?"

"Don't be silly." She drew a fingernail across his chest and when she zinged his nipple he decided the argument had concluded. "Just remember, this is to help you. You can control the blood hunger, Michael. But you've got to want to."

"I do want to."

"As much as you want me?"

"Chain me up, baby. Let's get this party started."

Turns out the chains were mighty comfortable. Michael didn't even notice his restraints as Jane's lips glided up from his belly, and over his chest. His stomach muscles tightened and every part of him strained for release. To capture the wicked and drink it in.

The clink of chain links had ceased to bother him. Now the only sound was the rhythm of Jane's heart-beat and the song of her desire.

An electric fire followed in the wake of her slippery, sliding kiss. A stroke across his nipple forged a longing moan from him. The excruciating pleasure sparked out to his extremities so, he felt he must give off light like some kind of firefly. Sweet flame consumed his entire body, making him feel alive, so alive.

She pressed a kiss to his mouth. Kir perfumed her breath, sweet, smooth cherry wine, just like Jane. Her body snugged against his, promising so much, and he knew she wouldn't deny him. The woman wasn't the sort to lay out treats, and then pull them away just as he reached for them.

Not that he could reach for them now.

Yes, he trusted her. Nothing in this world made him happier than to simply stand before her, taking in her dark, rich aura. And her magic.

Unsure how the actual transference of the magic occurred, Michael sucked in deeply, opening himself to every part of her.

"I'm a long way from mastering spells," she whispered. "But I'm working wishcraft on you right now."

"What are you wishing for?" He nudged his erection against her groin. "Isn't this enough for you?"

"Plenty. That's why I'm wishing your desire for need to stay dormant."

"Don't feel too terribly hungry right—ohhh."

"You're so hard. I don't know if I can climb up on you with you up against the wall like this. Oh, Michael."

"Jane, I want to be inside you. Right now. I can't do it in chains."

"You're right. This isn't going to work."

"No, it's working. All I want is you. Your sex wrapped around me." Firm, exploring fingers stretched him tightly. It was enough to make a man do what he had to do. "Promise I'll behave. But—"

Michael strained against the manacle on his left wrist. He pulled, the chain snapping taut. The bolts in the wall jiggled.

"Michael, wait there's a key!"

"No time. Don't let go of me. We're almost there, Jane. Just one more…tug."

The bolts gave free. Michael's arm swung out and he stepped up to catch the ends of the chain so they wouldn't slap Jane. He'd worry about a key later.

In no time he had Jane pressed to the wall, and lifted her leg to wrap around his hip. He didn't need both hands. And he'd lost all patience. And so he plunged into her and they came together.

He clung to her for the longest time, listening to her slowing breaths, following her heartbeats and they settled and began the usual rhythm inside him. Perspiration moistened her hair at her temple. He nuzzled there, loving the salty aroma of her skin.

Without releasing her, he tugged at the chain that still secured one of his arms. No exertion. It pulled free. A chunk of cement swung at the end of the chain, and he moved his arm to the side and set it on the floor so she wouldn't trip.

"That's incredible, Michael."

He shrugged. Sure, his strength had increased. Wasn't like it was magic.

"You could have done that earlier? When we were having sex?"

"Probably." Probably. And yet he'd been too distracted to attempt it. He should have been able to twist these manacles off and take control of their coming together. To pin her against the wall with both hands and thrust into her over and over, even after the first climax.

What kind of man had he become? Was she becoming stronger than him? He had never allowed a woman to control him. And he wasn't about to begin now.

"Michael. Should we go again?"

"Not interested." He stepped around, collecting his clothes, dragging the cement chunks along with him. "You just want to increase your magic anyway."

"What? Michael, how dare—"

He swung around. "Enough," he hissed. "I've had enough for now. Go get the key."

She left silently, and he was pleased. No, she wouldn't control him.

Chapter 17

Michael drove off in the Mini, without word to her. Fine, Jane thought.

She completely understood now when her mother would get upset with her father for his arrogant, demanding ways. It was as if they felt they walked slightly above all others. Of course, it could be the vampire/witch thing. Witches felt superior to vamps, and vice versa. Or was it a male/female thing?

Jane wasn't feeling superior, just lucky. If not a little cautious. She had never been afraid of magic before, because she couldn't use it. But now... What if she couldn't command it so skillfully as her mother did? Would she make a terrible mistake? How to reverse a spell gone bad? She had so much to learn!

Wandering out to the garden in the long periwinkle slip dress she'd donned after they'd made love, Jane bent over the fountain to inspect it. The water had stopped flowing. She located the motor housing, but it required lifting the bowl off to get at it, and it was far too heavy to even attempt.

"Hmm." On the other hand. Who needed a raging, muscle-bound vampire?

So far, she had only to think for something to happen and it did. Wishcraft. So she focused on the inner workings of the fountain, envisioning the flow of water up through the plastic piping and spewing––

"Yes!" Water splashed out of the angel's mouth, and splattered Jane's hands. "Now this could come in handy."

Why did the one man she cared about act like he could care less about this significant event in her life? That she could use her magic, after living one hundred and twenty five years without touching it was nothing less than remarkable.

And she owed it all to Michael.

Sitting on the grass right there at the circumference of the fountain, she crossed her legs, and caught her forehead in her palms.

"Well, Jane, what are you going to do now?" She was a nomad. She took lovers. She fell in lust. But never love. Having sex with a vampire? That was good. And he hadn't lost control last night.

But it didn't mean love. Did it?

For a very long time, life had been blessedly uncomplicated.

So how had a man, the complete and utter opposite of herself—why, a *vampire*—been able to capture her soul so easily?

It mattered to Jane what happened to Michael. She wanted him to master the darkness within himself so that material success could be possible. And she wanted to protect him from the stalkers and tribes and other shadows that lurked in hopes of stealing the last few morsels of his innocence.

Like you, Jane? Don't you want a piece of that innocence?

Sometimes her conscience could be so honestly cruel. And this time it spoke with Ravin's voice. For no matter the wonders that came to her, Jane could not ignore the ritual much longer. She had but days. And still no source to be found.

Save the one stripping you naked nightly.

Brushing away the thin ribbons of grass clinging along her bare legs, Jane sighed. She did reconnaissance on the garden. No bees buzzing about.

Had Michael become like the bees? Compelled to her, yet unable to hurt her beyond a few quick stings?

She had lied to him about having had a boyfriend. Decades earlier, Jane had walked away from a man she had truly loved. Guy had been in her life for sixteen years. Never once had he questioned her parents or her unflagging youth. And when finally he had? She'd freaked, leaving him without word and rushing back to the bitter sanctity of her father's arms. Much easier to run away from the truth than to face it.

And yet, she'd given Michael her truth without second thought. Now that was curious.

"You really are in love, you crazy woman."

"Okay, so you like him," she argued with her conscience. "Love? Maybe. Could be. Probably. He's so sexy. He is so—" Alive. Frenetic. Exciting. "And he's a great lover." And their sex gave her an undeniable boon. "But what will I do with him in ten years? Twenty?"

If he survived that long. The fact he hadn't bitten her yet was nothing less than remarkable.

Her mother and father had made immortality— and marriage vows—work. Not that Jane would ever consider marriage. Domestic pairing belonged in the same category as babies—she had no interest. But she had to look at what the future would bring if she intended to allow Michael into her life. It wasn't as though he'd die soon and she could go on to the next lover. This man would ever remain her peer—that is, if she completed the immortality ritual.

"Can you do it, Jane?"

"What's that?"

Now that was a familiar voice. Elation pressing her up to her feet and twisting her around, Jane skipped across the grass to land in the arms of her father. He lifted her feet from the ground in a generous bear hug and spun her once.

"Jane, dearest, you're always so wild when I see you." He looked her up and down. "Do you ever wear shoes?"

"Daddy! Why didn't you tell me you had plans to visit? I would have— Oh, you look so good. I can't believe it's been but a year. I miss you like it's been ten."

Indeed, Baptiste Rénan did cut a figure. Pushing up dark sunglasses onto the crown of his head, he drew her into the shadows edging the back of the house and then stood back to display the tailored charcoal suit he wore. Armani, no doubt, for Jane knew he favored the Italian designers. An elegant hint of pale green shirt peeked out between the lapels. Celadon, his favorite color. Any observer would remark he looked like Jane's peer, so little the centuries had done to age his face. Yet he'd trimmed his long dark hair to a stylish, over-the-ear swish that looked short in the back.

"Did mother finally convince you to cut your hair?"

"She cut it," he said with a sly smirk. Clasping Jane's hands he held out her arms to look her over. "Ever the earth child, my Jane. When will I finally get you into diamonds and cashmere?"

"Oh, Daddy, save your riches for mother. She adores it when you drown her in pretty things. I simply value the time I can spend with the two of you. How did you find me?"

"I called the local hardware store," Baptiste said as he draped an arm around Jane's waist and hugged her. "They gave me directions."

"But why now? What's up?"

"I received a most disturbing phone call last night. From a witch."

"Oh no, Ravin?"

He nodded. "She seems to think you've fallen for a source, darling."

"Oh, Daddy." No, Jane wanted to say, but she'd never been good at lying to her father. But the pride shining in her father's eyes made her hold her tongue. "It's complicated."

"I bet."

Baptiste ran his palms over the stained glass sections arrayed on the plywood worktable. "This color here."

"Celadon. Your favorite." Jane leaned over his shoulder as he traced the pale green curve that formed the underside of a stylized leaf. "I always include that color in my designs. Makes me feel like you and mother are here watching over me."

He reached back and squeezed her hand. "You are so talented, dearest daughter of mine. Mother insists we spare the windows in the upper bedroom suite for your imagination to run wild. Will you do it?"

"You needn't ask. I've another job following this one in the fall, but I'm sure I can be in Venice by spring."

"Jane, Jane. And you call me a type-A. You're the one with a schedule she must check before fitting her own family into it! Will you come stay with your mother and I? Write down *family* on your mental calendar. Fun. Conversation. Can you do that? Simply…relax?"

She couldn't help but smirk. Her father was out

of touch with her lifestyle. "All I do is relax, Daddy. It's not as if my work is strenuous. If anything, I need excitement."

"You know your mother and I can give you that. Carnivale! Oh, yes, you must make it to Venice for carnivale. I'll order a fabulous costume for you and have Esmeralda make the mask. It'll sparkle with diamonds and emeralds to match your eyes. Don't say no."

"Yes."

"So easy as that?" Baptiste kissed both her cheeks and her forehead. "Dearest Jane. I'll have your room made up in that splendid Indian motif you adore, and beads and fringe everywhere, along with frocked paper for the walls and pillows and rich, lush fabrics."

"Daddy, a simple bed will do."

A comical cringe moved his mouth. The man had ever been a fop, and he wasn't afraid to fully live his swishiness. An attribute that had once attracted Jane's mother to the man, and still did.

"Very well," she conceded. "Some rich fabrics. And if you must know, I like my pillows squishy, not hard."

"I'll order half a dozen squishy pillows for the princess's chambers," he drawled in that lovely French lilt he never tried to lose. "Mother will be so delighted. She's been rather bored lately. Every day I must conjure a new experience to keep her occupied. Did I mention your mother got a tattoo?"

"What? Daddy, she didn't?"

"She did. On her back, very low and just above her—"

"Don't even say it. My mother? It was because you asked her, I suppose."

"Not at all. She's been engaged in a wicked flirtation with a local artist. Well, you know we must have our flirtations after all these years."

"It must be difficult at times to maintain a relationship for so long."

"Not at all. Flirtations, darling."

"Don't tell me any more, Daddy. I want to keep you and mother's love chaste in my heart, if you don't mind."

"It is, and always will be, a monogamous relationship. Promise."

He'd removed his suit jacket and the celadon shirt looked a piece of the garden.

"Now." Baptiste tapped his bottom lip, concerned. "This source Ravin called me about. While I'm pleased you've made plans for the ritual, I fear they are not the kind of plans I'm expecting. Who, what, when, where and why?"

"His name is Michael Lynsay, and he's staying here at the house. Has been since I arrived. I invaded his privacy, actually."

"Oh? You stumbled upon a source? Jane, in all your years, you've been very careful to avoid the strange."

Boy, had she been careful. And she liked that she could not offend her father with her tendency to label all things supernatural strange.

Yet, rarely did her father come out and say the word—vampire. He had the utmost respect for the term, but it was like a white man calling himself a Caucasian in casual conversation.

"Trust me, I didn't search this out. Michael is in the same band as the owner of this house."

"I see. I suppose that was a coup, you needing a source."

"It's not like that. In fact, I think I…"

"*Mon Dieu,* Jane, was the witch right? Are you and this singer an item?"

An item. How her father moved so sinuously with the times and the ever-changing slang never ceased to impress her.

"I do care about Michael."

Bowing his head, Baptiste studied the floor. "The century mark has arrived," he stated. "One hundred years ago this month you performed the immortality ritual, Jane. The full moon is but two nights away."

Two nights. And what else had she been thinking about lately that was to arrive so quickly?

"Need I remind you, you must perform the ritual once every century to maintain immortality?"

No, he need not. The ritual was the most distasteful experience known to Jane, and to think about doing it again prickled up goose bumps over her arms and neck. And yet, she had no compunction toward it. Only, Michael must not be involved. No way.

"I…" A startling chord of dread strummed in her brain, as tangible as a plucked guitar string. How to be truthful with her father? A man who had only ever wanted what was good and just for her? "I'm not sure…"

"Jane, dearest, there's no time for dawdling." Baptiste crossed the floor and took her shoulders in his hands. "That vampire is your only hope for continued immortality. Why, for continued breath! You need him."

"But Father—"

Baptiste sucked in a breath and let it out slowly. Lowering his head, he looked up through his lashes at her. Whiskied honey, the color her mother had once used to describe her father's eyes. Brilliant and all seeing. But they were soft now.

"Jane, do you love this vampire?"

She could but nod. To voice her feelings would cement the betrayal to her father's expectations. And to even mention they'd been making love and sharing the magic?

"I see." He sighed heavily. "Then allow me to put this out into the air, shall I? What sort of love would it be, *could* it be, if, in two days—should you not complete the ritual—you died? How then will you love the vampire?"

"Daddy, that's hardly fair—"

"No, but it is something you must consider. You are living on stolen time, Jane."

Yes, but to survive, and maintain her immortality? Had she any right to take another person's life to prolong her own? Oh, how to argue this impossible choice? And why, suddenly, did she want to argue it?

She knew why. Love! Look at the mess it had put her in.

"Jane, listen to me. There's no room for infatuation or even simple kindness. In two days you must sacrifice Michael Lynsay."

Chapter 18

Michael pulled the Mini up the gravel road. A rental car sat in the driveway. Hmm… Couldn't be the vigilante witch; she rode that kick-ass chopper. He didn't believe Jane had any other friends in the area, but maybe he was wrong.

With a shopping bag in one hand, and a bouquet of freesia in the other, Michael strode inside. He couldn't wait to crush the ridiculously fragrant orange blooms into Jane's hair as he lay next to her in bed. And whisper an apology for his macho posturing earlier.

So he was strong and tough and could tell a woman what to do; didn't mean he should treat her with disrespect.

A leather briefcase lay on the kitchen table, a digital lock gleaming brightly above the handle. His senses cringed, and his teeth tingled.

"Michael, we're upstairs!"

He made a beeline for the upper-floor workroom and couldn't find his voice when he found a Hollywood-good-lookin' young man in a fitted suit standing next to his Jane.

Fangs tingling in their sockets, he lowered his hand, the flowers slipping along his fingers, but he crunched the stems tightly before they fell to the floor.

"I see you've done some shopping," Jane said as she approached him. "For me?" She lifted the flowers and waved them under her nose.

"Who the hell is that?" Michael hissed lowly.

"Calm the bravado," she whispered.

An inhale forced the downward motion of his teeth to stop.

Jane took his hand and walked him over to the man waiting near the worktable. "Michael, this is Baptiste Rénan. My father. Daddy, Michael Lynsay."

Her father? Relief scurried up his neck. Michael dropped the shopping bag and slapped his hand into Baptiste's offered hand to shake it vigorously. The shimmer snaked a vibrant shock up his arm.

"A pleasure to meet you, Mr. Rénan. Your daughter has told me a little about you. But knowing you're one of my kind makes it all good. Did Jane know you were coming to visit?"

Baptiste tugged his hand from Michael's grip and inserted it in his front trouser pocket. "I tend to surprise my daughter with visits, because she makes it supremely impossible to communicate with her no-electronics nonsense. Myself, I'd go absolutely over the moon without my trusty BlackBerry."

"I'm suffering electronic withdrawal myself. Good thing there's a studio here, I'd be lost without music."

"Yes, music." Baptiste flicked a glance to Jane but Michael couldn't tear his eyes from the man. Another vampire. And so normal! He wore a three-piece suit, for cripes sake. "My wife and I enjoy all styles of music, though we've never been successful in developing Jane's appreciation for opera or that delicious country style."

"Jane tells me you live in Venice?"

"And you in California?"

"Wherever the road takes me. But I do have a mansion in Los Angeles."

"So why Minnesota right now?"

Michael shrugged. "A little R and R. Did Jane tell you?"

"I haven't had much time to chat with Daddy." Jane slipped her arm into Michael's crooked arm. A subtle anxiety held her stiffly as she pressed her body alongside his thigh and shoulder, yet her heartbeat remained calm. "He's not here for long. Just come to tease me."

"Jane." Her father mocked a pout. "I never tease, and am always most serious about my reasons for anything I should ask of you."

Something tightened the tension between the

two of them. Michael would have to be dead to miss that feeling. And he wasn't undead.

"Can you stay the night?" he wondered. "I'd love to talk with you…"

About living with a witch. How to make that situation work? And to control the jealousy he felt at her growing power? But he wasn't sure he should reveal yet that he'd been sleeping with the man's daughter. And try as he might, he couldn't get a read on Jane.

"I have so many questions." He spread out his arms to encompass the enormity of his need. "Please, Mr. Rénan, will you stay?"

"I'm so sorry, Michael. Much as I'd love to chat, I must plead leave."

"But you just got here." He turned to Jane, still her expression gave him nothing. "There's plenty of room for you to stay. There's even a coffin in the basement if you prefer—"

Baptiste's dark brows rose at mention of the coffin.

"Once Daddy makes up his mind, he's decided," Jane said. "I suppose I should walk you out," she said to her father. "Shall we?"

Michael felt the tension slide from his arm as Jane left his side, and he watched her cross the floor behind her father. Everything about her had changed. Stiff, not relaxed. Blank. As if she were purposefully trying to keep something from him.

Had he walked in on an argument? Why would the man fly all the way from Venice to see his daughter for so short a time? He couldn't have been here any more than two hours, for Michael had only been out for three.

He followed them, and when the twosome reached the front door, Baptiste turned to again shake Michael's hand and wish him well. "It was good to meet you, Michael. *Adieu!*"

Jane kissed Michael on the chin. "Stay here. I'm going to walk my father out."

Catching his fingers on the trim over the door, Michael stood there, fighting the urge to follow them outside.

There was something secretive about the pair. They weren't about to allow him into their world. Jane's composure had so altered he couldn't be sure what to think of Baptiste. Was her apparent devotion to him because it was demanded?

She turned to Michael as they stopped beside the rental car. *Don't watch.*

So Michael closed the door and pounded his forehead against the jamb, once, twice.

"Don't leave me."

Jane looked to the ground, wistful as her father kissed her cheek and hugged her. She knew he had plans to stay in Minneapolis; nothing but a five-star hotel would satisfy him. Yet, there was no way he'd leave town until after the full moon.

"I can't do it," she said. "I love him."

"So quickly?"

"Yes." Oh, yes, she had never meant the word so

much. "And I won't listen to arguments against love at first sight because I remember well you said the very same thing about mother. Can't you see beyond the rock star facade? Michael thinks only of me, and he would never harm me."

"You said he hasn't control of his blood hunger. How can you know he won't attack you without volition? And then what? The man you love will become ash." Baptiste snapped his fingers. "Like that. Gone. So much for your endearing love. And if not him? Well then, you'll be the one who suffers for this dreadful fascination."

"Daddy, don't do this. Please. When have you ever known me to confess love for a man?"

"Frequently. And always at the beginning of a relationship. I do recall that one man who danced at the Moulin Rouge—what was his name?"

"Daddy."

"That first night you were ready to run away with him to the exotic locale of China to raise babies and cook rice." Baptiste mocked a horrified shiver. "Jane, you are infatuated with yet another bohemian musician who has no care, morals or goals. Admit it. Like a teenager, you've never grown beyond that lust-rush one gets upon discovering a new lover. You need that vampire. He is your only source! It was not meant to be."

"You don't know that."

"You've had sex with him, haven't you."

"Daddy!" This was not a conversation she was willing to have with her father.

"You know what will happen, Jane. If he can control his hunger for the blood, and successfully make love to you, he then steals away what little magic you have within you. Don't do it, Jane. Don't give away your magic to that idiot."

"I can give my magic to whomever I please. And look at you? You must take from mother every time the two of you—" No, she couldn't say it; she never talked about sex with her father.

"It's different between the two of us, Jane. We shared blood at my creation, so it's not the same. I cannot enslave your mother through the sex magic, nor would I wish to. But that vampire." He thrust an angry finger toward the house. "He'll take advantage of you."

"And what if he's giving something to me?"

"Like what?"

Jane chewed her lower lip. The magic had grown; it was beginning to develop. No, she couldn't tell her father, not until she was more confident and sure it would stick around. And if she did reveal it, he'd whisk her immediately to Venice to show her mother and begin her education, without concern for her completing the job, let alone leaving Michael behind.

"He gives me love, Daddy. And I simply won't do it. I will not sacrifice Michael to prolong my own life!"

Baptiste stepped up to Jane and toyed with the ends of her hair, listing in the breeze. He did not smile, nor did he meet her gaze.

"What ever happened to 'and ye harm none'?" she asked.

He smirked. Well, it wasn't *his* saying. "It would be impossible to find another source within two days."

She wanted to let him know that Ravin was looking, but would the witch be successful?

"Jane, haven't you had your fill of artists and musicians? The man is a needy little bastard. And if you look beyond all that…he is a vampire. I've always thought you very much against my kind."

"Don't say that. I love you, Daddy. I've just always strived for the normal."

"And Michael Lynsay is normal? Jane, the boy—and yes, he is but a boy, especially in the greater scheme of immortality and life everlasting—is a spoiled, arrogant rock star."

"No, he's driven. And yes, a bit cocky, but you are exactly the same. Don't you see? Oh!"

"What? Jane?"

Stunned by a sudden realization, Jane pressed a hand over her pounding heartbeats. "I've fallen in love with a man who is exactly like my father."

Baptiste puffed up his chest proudly. "He is nothing like me."

"Put a frock coat on him, and slip a microphone in your hand, and I wouldn't be able to determine the two of you from one another. Oh, Daddy, just leave. I can't do this! I won't!"

Her father lifted her chin. In the evening twilight, his honey brown eyes sought her so fiercely she was swept back to childhood when he'd admonish her after running the streets shoeless, and in her fine silk stockings.

This man was home, her heart and her safety. But it seemed they'd been playing the teenager seeks a boyfriend against her father's wishes act for far too many decades. Would he never grant her the freedom her wild soul craved?

Was that it? Always she had run back to her father's arms after a disastrous relationship. When would she finally break free?

"You mustn't sacrifice your life for a fleeting love affair, Jane."

"Wh-what happens if I don't perform the ritual?"

"Instead of aging gracefully, all those stolen years will swoop in to destroy you."

"That's— Are you sure? It sounds so wildly remarkable. Like something from a fiction novel."

"Oh? As we vampires have been relegated to the pages? So much for your charmed life, dearest one."

Sniffing back a tear, Jane surprised herself with such sudden emotion. It wasn't because her father had admonished her. And though a hug from her mother would feel right, she didn't need that affection this instant.

In truth, she knew the tears were because she didn't want to lose *him*.

Neither did she wish to consider her own swift death. Though she'd been granted far longer on this earth than any mortal should have, she'd grown to accept it, and wasn't prepared to consider it suddenly ending.

"Jane." Her father pressed his cheek beside hers. The comfort of his hug didn't do it this time.

Just set me free. Let my rebellions put me where they will.

And yet, all she had ever done was to rebel. For a hundred years. Was it time to straighten up? To respect her father's demands?

"Do not leave this world, precious one," Baptiste whispered in her ear. "Take your life, Jane. Take it!"

Chapter 19

Michael waited as the software reloaded onto the iPod. Jesse had shipped it overnight express. The FedEx truck had just delivered it.

Jane had sequestered herself in a hot tub last night, immediately after her father had left. And she had risen hours earlier and went straight to the studio, without peeking in on him. He'd give her space. Wait for her to come to him. At least, for a few impatient hours. After that, all bets were off.

He missed the woman, and the feeling was surmounted by the fact that she was right there, so close, yet so untouchable. She pulsed inside him. And yet, no amount of flowers, scattered, bouqueted, or climbing the walls could cure what bothered her soul.

And what hurt her, hurt him. It was almost as if he could feel her sorrow. The monster didn't like it, and the man desperately wanted to change it, to shake the pain away from her soul.

The software loaded successfully, and he began to search the videos. The first title was merely a string of As. Not one of his entries. He clicked it. Again the face flashed before him for no more than two seconds.

Pale long hair obscured half the female face. Her mouth opened, as if she were speaking, but even with the earbuds, there was no sound. A flicker of hand brushed across her hair and— Video static.

His heartbeat stalled in his chest, Michael clasped his shirt. "It can't be. It looks so much like her."

Who could know this image would disturb him? How?

There was no clue attached to the short video clip, not even an icon with a brief description. Once more he played the ten-second flash. And once more he sucked in his breath at the sight of her.

He scanned through the other files, the podcasts, photos and songs—all there. Nothing new. The addresses. Wait—he hadn't put that entry there. Banks. Sylvan Banks.

The name Jane said the kid from the club gave her. The same kid from the graveyard? Was he really a reporter? Looked young, but that didn't mean a thing. He had admitted to having a camera in his car.

Michael read the details of the entry. It was an address in Clear Rapids, a suburb just south of North

Lake. No phone number or email listed. Above the address it read To find me:

"Well."

Someone was playing a game, hoping to lure him.

Thing is, did that someone realize they might hook a vampire? And if they did, would it be safe for Michael?

Jane snapped a piece of ivory glass and held the shape of a skull before her for inspection, while her thoughts drifted forward a few days.

She didn't want to perform the ritual.

And she did.

Performed once every century, it ensured her immortality. Only trouble was, a source was required. Source meaning, a vampire. And after all was chanted, promised and sacrificed, there usually wasn't much vampire left to argue. The dark ones had a different word for their unfortunate compatriots chosen to be a source—ash.

If you ever need a thing, I'm there.

A promise from Ravin Crosse, issued decades ago after Jane had first met her. After watching vampires slaughter her parents, when but a child in eighteenth-century Bulgaria, that girl had no sympathy for any bloodsucker.

The trouble? Getting a source was impossible if the witch couldn't find a vampire. Jane was a little surprised. Ravin had claimed to have the Sight, and she'd seen the evidence of that boon. So where were all the vamps?

She laid the skull next to the swatch of emerald glass that formed a grass blade. Was it selfish to extend one's life by means of a spell, trickery and magic?

"Yes, it is selfish," she muttered. But it was all that she knew.

She had been born into this world from two other-worldly beings. Not a moment of her life had been spent *not* knowing all things were possible. The world was populated—albeit secretly, and sometimes not so very secretly—by many who were inhuman or immortal, and those that were close to human, but not.

Werewolves loped across the lands. They could be found in every country, forest and territory. Vampires, yes they stalked the shadows, surviving under the radar, and because of the ridiculous acceptance mortals wore as a mask.

As for faeries and trolls, and others of the Folk, Jane had crossed paths with a few in her travels. Faeries were as varied and particular as the human race. She'd once dated one, but had decided his attraction to her would never grow stronger than his desire for absinthe. Elves, well, they were a regal breed and rarely associated on mortal grounds.

Not to say this earth was composed entirely of mortal ground. So many more places were of the other realms, most often bastardized and stolen for mortal use over the centuries. That is how they became myth. Because the mortals stopped seeing them.

Walking that line of non-sight and daring suited Jane perfectly. For all purposes she was merely mortal. Yet immortal.

Unless, she choose to not go through with the ritual.

What if your life ends suddenly? Pouf, you are gone?

And yet, to live, for Michael, may be the first unselfish act she had ever considered.

Why had she allowed herself to care about a man who should have been nothing more than a tool to her?

"Jane?"

Approaching slowly, Michael padded across the floor, barefoot. Skinny, faded jeans wrapped his powerful limbs, and the shirt, decorated with skulls, seemed a little tight. Had his clothes shrunk?

"What's wrong?" he asked.

"Not sure. Did that shirt shrink?"

He stretched his arm, bending the tight fabric at the elbow. "I wore this the other night and it was fine. It's weird, but I think I'm…growing."

She smirked. "You don't realize it's the magic, do you?"

"Magic is making my clothes smaller?"

"You're growing stronger, Michael. Gaining muscle and, probably soon, will be popping those seams."

He slapped a hand over his chest and did a knee bend that did indeed tear at the seams. "Guess I'll have to pick up some clothes when I'm in town."

"You leaving now?"

"Yes, there's…something I need to do."

"Could you stop by a hardware store and get me some copper striping? I've run out."

"Sure. So um…everything all right with you?"

She sensed where he wanted to go with that

question. Since her father had left for the city, Jane had been avoiding Michael. How to look him in the eye knowing what needed to be done?

"Everything is going to be fine, Michael. I've been trying to catch up since the window broke. Sorry, if you feel like I've been avoiding you."

"You sure it doesn't have anything to do with your father?"

"Not at all." Truth, or as close to truth as she was willing to give. "We just see each other so rarely lately. For as long as I've lived, you'd think I'd get over my homesickness."

"I understand. You've been around longer than I have. That's right, you said 1881. You know…" He trailed a tickling finger along her arm. "I like dating an older woman. The guys in the band will get a kick out of this."

"Are we dating? Does one date when they share the same house? I thought we were…"

"What?"

"I don't know." She moved a piece of glass on the table, which slid her arm from his touch. "Just lovers, I suppose."

"Like that? *Just* lovers. Like…just cheese. Or just grass." He crossed his arms over his chest. "What's with you, Jane? I know something is bothering you. Is it me? Don't you like me?"

"I adore you, Michael."

"Then why so cool today?"

"I'm not being cold, am I?" *Yes, you are!* "I, we…well, what are we exactly?"

"Lovers." He kissed her. "Friends." Another kiss. "Family, of a sort. We're both part of the world of darkness."

"I'm not one of the dark. I quite enjoy the light."

"I see. So it's fine to take a vampire as a lover, but you'll never love him, or consider him proper boyfriend material. Heaven forbid he should drool blood on you, or vamp out and actually bite you."

"I don't do boyfriends, Michael. Never have." Well, there had been that one, regrettable time…

"In over a hundred years, you've never had a boyfriend?"

"Think about it. It's not very practical for a woman who will live forever to get attached to one man for any length of time. As I continue to thrive and experience the world, never changing, those around me grow old and die."

"You've never had a true love?"

She shook her head, but looked away from his delving gaze. Some lies were necessary, if only to keep back the regret and tears. "What is true love, really? Just an ideal. Nothing solid."

"I'm not going anywhere, Jane." He swept an arm around her waist and diverted her attention into his eyes. There, she saw honesty, and a hunger for truth. "Don't you want to take a chance on me?"

The truth rushed up unbidden. "Yes, I—I actually do. But don't push it, please. I need to take every day one step at a time. I…I prefer my lovers uncomplicated." Now that was a lie. "Can you understand that?"

"I'm about as complicated as they come."

"No kidding." And more interesting for it. "Don't give me that sexy look. Save it for your fans."

"Fine. Truth?"

"All right. Truth. You want to know how I feel about you?" Could she speak her true feelings for him? It was a bold challenge. But like this whole mistake, it was a challenge thrown down, and must be taken. "I think I'm falling in love with you."

"Seriously?"

"I'm—"

"—always serious," he finished for her, with a knowing grin.

"What about you?"

"That's easy. I fell in love the moment I saw you standing in the bedroom holding that deadly box cutter. Your eyes were wild and alive. Your hair, it was angry with me. Every part of you tempts the monster, Jane, and every other part calms it. What did I do to deserve you?"

Not a thing. There was no fate, or deserving involved. "We both got lucky, I guess."

"I don't believe in luck. I've seen too much to believe in it."

"So you've seen it all? Please." She pushed from his embrace and paced around to the end of the worktable. "It doesn't matter how long you've been around," she said over her shoulder. "Or what you've seen. It's all in what you believe."

"Fine." Embracing her from behind, and tugging the cutting tool from her fingers, he clasped her hands within his wide strong grip. "I believe in us, Jane. Don't be afraid of it. Whatever you should ask of me, I will give to you. No matter what."

Tucking her head down, Jane kissed his hand and closed her eyes. Whatever she should ask? He couldn't begin to imagine the dreaded favor a witch could ask of a vampire.

Michael drove the Mini to Maple Street. Tipping his sunglasses from his forehead onto his nose, he then surveyed the area.

After the burn he'd gotten a few days ago out in the back yard, he didn't want to tempt fate again, so he tugged up his shirt to cover his face and ears. A new shirt; he'd stopped at a strip mall on the way. He'd gone from a large to an extra large—simply by having sex with Jane.

Nice. And he was pretty sure *everything* had increased in size, not just the muscles on his arms and legs.

He strode swiftly up the sidewalk, his boot chains clanking until he reached the safety of the shadows before the house.

Old newspapers littered the stoop of the small green stucco house. Michael scanned the front of the property. The windows were darkened with sunscreen plastic and shades were pulled over that. Shrubs were overgrown and the grass was badly in need of a mow.

After five rings of the doorbell, Michael decided to walk around the side of the house to look for a back entrance. Clinging to the shadows he stalked through the grass.

The screen door rattled and sprang free from the doorframe as if it had been sealed there with paint for centuries. Michael whipped back around to the front steps.

Someone studied him from the shadows of the interior. Michael couldn't make out features but he did smell something chemical ooze out from inside.

"Wondering when you would stop by," the person inside said. "Enter, vampire, freely and of your own will."

Smirking at the theatrics—and yet his heart pounded at the very gall of the invitation—this kid *knew*—Michael pushed in the screen and gripped the guy's shoulders. He pinned him to the wall behind the door and slammed him so roughly he heard bones clack.

"Who the hell are you?"

"You found me," the reporter offered, calm enough for a man restrained. "Sylvan Banks. You must have found the address and tracked me down. Get your facts straight, will ya?"

"I will get *you* straight if you don't watch your mouth. What's your deal? I've never done anything to you. I don't even know you." He gave another shove. Banks. He was the one from the graveyard. And he wasn't a kid, but he did still have the acne and gawky build. "Why'd you steal my iPod?"

"Didn't steal it. Found it in the graveyard."

"You tampered with it."

"Wanted you to find me. And now you have, vampire. Let me go."

"The vampire is a myth." Michael slammed him hard, then released him and strode into the dank shadows of a living room.

But a tatty couch and glass-topped coffee table sat before an old television that looked something out of a *Leave It to Beaver* rerun. The air in the place was not right. Musty. It didn't feel lived in. "Who the hell are you?"

"I was hired to verify your condition and bring you to my mistress."

"Verify my—" Anger curdled in Michael's gut like a virus. He had to remain calm. Jane's soft touch was too far away to still the wanting rage.

"Who hired you, and why lure me through some idiot kid? What do you want? Money? You know, after all the roadies, managers and lawyers have been paid, there ain't a lot left to be divided between the five band members."

"I've been given enough money that I don't need to ask for any from you. But you're right, Michael, there is a purpose to my madness."

"It's Mr. Lynsay to you."

Banks scrubbed a palm over his tousled hair. "I don't give a shit who or what you are. But my mistress does."

"Mistress?" What kind of nutty fantasy was he playing in? "Give me a name."

"You will know her when you see her."

"Her?"

Banks tapped a finger against his thin lips, but his eyes couldn't hide the smile he sought to cover.

"Step back, you're starting to piss me off. And if you touch me—" Michael inhaled, the move drawing him taller, and stretching back his shoulders. "Don't get me riled, that wouldn't be a smart move."

Anger remained at bay—barely. Michael wouldn't vamp out on this man. It wasn't worth the energy. He'd controlled the monster before, with Jane, he could do it now, without her.

"Of course, because the vampire is a wild, unpredictable beast." Banks snarled and made a ridiculous clawing motion to illustrate his accusation. "I know that. I've dealt with you bastards before." He flicked his finger behind the neck of his shirt and a glint of metal popped out.

Michael flinched at sight of the small gold cross.

"Figured a guy like you would have been baptized." Banks patted the cross, content it served a purpose without having to wield it. "Like I said, my mistress is the one who wants you, not me. Let me introduce you to her, then maybe I can get the bloodsucking bitch off my back."

Fitting his open palm against the idiot's neck, Michael shoved him into the wall and easily lifted his body inches from the floor. Yes, his fangs were down. And yes, the cross burned.

"I'm not about to trust you farther than I can toss you. What's her name?"

"Isabelle LaPierre" came a voice from the next room.

Michael dropped the reporter. The burn on his hand smoked. His entire body went rigid at that voice.

The voice of his blood master. The woman for whom he'd waited decades.

Chapter 20

Yes, decades. He had always opened the door to a knock, expectant, hopeful that she had returned. She was never there. He'd answered the phone, listening for her voice. No such luck.

He'd turned away woman after woman, some far more beautiful than she had been. Yet his bed simply remained empty, as unfulfilled as his heart. He had almost gone to ground a few decades ago, unwilling to stalk the night if he could not do it by her side.

No woman had ever attracted beyond the blood that she could give him. If it could not be her, then he had wanted no other.

Only after decades of this idiot behavior, had

Michael finally slipped out of it—and into an even more destructive habit. The quest for adrenaline.

Blood trickled down Michael's throat. A fine, acrid stream. He'd bitten the side of his tongue. Swallowing seemed an immense task.

Blood scent—no, *it's your own.* Michael shook off the urge to attack; yet it didn't dissipate, nor did he wish it to.

Attack? The impulse didn't feel right. It shouldn't be right.

A stream of weary evening sun entered a side window, and beamed across the bare hardwood floor. It stopped, as if a carpet of light, before a blue velvet sofa with curved wooden arms. Dust motes sifted in a deceptive barrier between Michael and the pale figure.

Before the sofa, she stood, her back to him, most of it revealed, for the low cut of the gown dipped to just above her hips.

Palest flesh-colored silk, dotted with shimmers of diamond, clung to her narrow, yet curvaceous figure. Her skin blended seamlessly with the fabric. Long hair cascaded like cream down the inviting slope of her bare back, and ended at the gentle rise of her derriere.

She looked over her shoulder, revealing but the left side of her face, not quite making eye contact. The pose was merely that, Michael presumed—a pose. He had seen this a thousand times before in the media. And he'd posed for enough pictures to know. Never reveal the complete picture; leave them wanting more.

But more than want, he wondered.

Why now?

La Belle Dame sans Merci had stepped back into his life. It had been his nickname for her. He'd given it to her, not because she was a merciless tyrant, but because she'd always wanted one more orgasm when they'd made love. One more, and then another, and another. So many she demanded, and mercilessly, she took from him. Not that he'd argued terribly much at the time.

But then she'd left him. In the worst possible manner.

Unexpectedly, Michael blinked at the bleary oblivion threatening his calm rationale.

Did merely standing in the same room with the woman who had created him do it? Could his blood sense hers? Well, of course. For now that he focused, he could feel her. Heartbeats racing like a hummingbird's. *Not like Jane.* So frenzied. She must be nervous. Good.

"It has been a while, Michael."

The voice, deep and calm—always a surprise coming from one so delicate—filled Michael's blood like whiskey to a recovering alcoholic's. They stood at too great a distance to touch, and yet, the shimmer traced Michael's veins in a speeding rush. He could feel her…everywhere, inside and out. Her blood pumped inside his veins. He had been her creation. She still whispered in his blood each time he fed.

"Isabelle." He said it with the hard long EE at the beginning, as she preferred it pronounced.

It had been decades since he'd put voice to that name, but not a day passed he didn't know her.

The beam of sun avoided her, but she needn't the light. Like a winter queen standing amidst the drudgery of a barren landscape, she shone. And her eyes were gold—the one he could see—like a cat's iris, surrounded by so much white. Eerie. Devastating.

Why did she not turn completely to face him?

"Do you forgive my absence?"

It was a ridiculous question. And he, wound up tightly like a spring, and utterly stunned, took it with a chuckle. Michael let out all the tension, shaking his shoulders and releasing his voice as if on stage.

"Forgive?" he barreled out. "Hmm, let's see?"

Pacing away from her, because he didn't want to look at the porcelain face that hadn't changed in five decades, Michael reeled through his thoughts. "We had an amazing affair that lasted six months. I lived only for your regard. In fact, I quit my job at the radio station so I could be at your beck and call. Every night at nine, there was Isabelle, standing in my doorway. Ready for sex. I suspected nothing. You didn't tell me a thing about yourself. And then when you decided to reveal all? You bit me, changed me to a vampire and said 'Have a nice life, lover.'"

He turned to find Isabelle's calm, unchanging stare. "Did I get all of that right?"

"You haven't changed, Michael. Still cocky and arrogant, and as full of yourself as ever. Yes, that's about right. But I never promised you forever. I had thought you'd be over it by now."

"I am completely over you, Isabelle. I haven't thought of you for decades."

"Not a day has passed that I haven't thought of you."

"You lie."

"You're still the most handsome man I've ever held in my arms."

He twisted his neck to cast her a grin. "I should hope so."

"I love your arrogance. Come, give me a kiss, will you?"

"Oh, I don't think so. I'm not going to fall back into the old rhythm, Isabelle. I have a life now. And it doesn't include you."

"Is she very pretty, then?"

"What?"

"Your life?"

"It's been decades. I've accomplished a lot. I have a marvelous life. I own property and have security for an endless future. And you can only guess it is a woman that fulfills me?"

"That's usually the case with you public personas. I suspect the vampire got lost behind the flash of camera bulbs and adoration. I've seen your music videos. The Fallen. What an appropriate name for a music group featuring a vampire as lead singer. You're very daring to put yourself out there before the masses like that. Aren't you afraid you'll be discovered?"

Michael sought her gaze for the threat that she held. If she wished, she could expose him. But not so wise, considering the source.

If he stepped closer, would he then step back into their rhythm? Already her heartbeat raced alongside his. Those furious, fast beats, always challenging, calling to him to meet the match, to dive into the excitement.

Michael reached out, his fingers grasping but air. Nothing there to touch. No not-witch to cling to for support.

But he didn't need Jane to help him now. What could she offer him? *Beyond the strength you've received from her magic? She offers you home, love and*—not the fiery adventure Isabelle had once given him. Jane could never stand next to Isabelle and outshine this woman's pale moon-light glow.

Plain Jane. But no longer, for she had gained real magic. Is that what troubled him lately? She was growing stronger, a match to him. Would she go beyond him? And then, would she no longer need him?

Isabelle brushed a hand down the side of her torso, smoothing gracefully across her hip. Slender, pale, a dream. The curl of her fingers drew attention to the curve of fabric cutting low upon her back. "I did so try to look presentable for you."

"You are lovely, as ever." Truly, she was. "But why now?" Michael asked. "Why did you wait so long to seek me out? Weren't you, at the very least, curious if I had survived, if I had learned to live as a vampire?"

"You have always been strong, Michael. I had no doubts you would rise to the challenge and flourish. As I see you have. You're flush with blood and I can smell your strength. You look so...virile. Michael, you're so much more than when we last met. Admit it, I gave you a great gift."

Fisting his fingers, he snarled and punched the air. "I will not breathe your lies!"

"I've no lies to give. Merely admiration."

More blood streamed down Michael's throat. He couldn't stop pacing, or wondering. Or looking. The woman drew his attention like a singer on the stage. Yet Isabelle needn't talent beyond the twinkle in her forged metal eyes and the tilt of her head. Wicked charm coaxed at him, so obviously twisted, and yet, alluring.

Slapping his palms together before him, Michael bowed his head to his thumbs and shook his head.

All right, so this was real. Like it or not, they were connected through blood.

"What do you want from me, Isabelle? You've had me followed. You've stalked me, obviously. It can't simply be that you've missed me."

"Come closer, and I'll tell you."

He should have replied that he didn't need to take a step to hear her, but instead Michael found himself walking toward her before the thought against it occurred.

Sunlight shimmered in Isabelle's hair, but still she did not stand directly in it. As he got closer to her, the scent of expensive perfume surrounded him. It was subtle, oriental, and exotic—like her.

"Look at me," he said. "Turn around, Isabelle."

Graceful as a dove, she turned, and twisted up her

head to look him directly. The movement was awkward, perhaps even painful for her to perform.

Michael gasped. The right side of her face was riddled with ugly red scars, the flesh puckered as if stripped away then, when moist with blood, it had settled there in that shape.

"Isabelle?"

"It's recent," she said, the regal tone to her voice softening. She tilted down her head so her hair swung over the tormented side of her face, but not completely. "From a witch. I was a very lucky. Most vampires never walk away from the death cocktail."

The magnitude of her confession struck Michael in his heart. Stalked by the horrors of his ugly reality. He gripped his chest, stepped back a few feet, and blew out his breath.

"Don't be frightened by me, Michael. I am still the woman you once made love to for days on end."

"I'm not frightened. I'm sorry for you. It's just…" He looked upon his future. His fate, should Jane's blood ever contact his flesh. And that was if he were lucky. "How? To survive?"

"She spat at me," Isabelle explained. "I am so… tired."

Now she sat on the blue velvet couch behind her, crossing her legs elegantly and leaning back, though she laid the scarred side of her face against the back of the couch.

"I was able to wipe away the blood with my clothing, but it was too late," she said. "The blood works very quickly. It burned long and so deep.

Right through to my mouth. It ate away half my teeth. It's been months. The inside of my mouth has healed, the teeth are coming back, but the outside... A burn from witch's blood is much different than one from the sun. No matter how much mortal blood I drink, it serves little toward the physical repairs I require."

"And how do you repair?" Oh, stupid question. The answer punched him in the gut.

"That is why I've come to you, Michael. I need your blood."

Of course it couldn't be something easy like a simple handshake.

And yet, to give her blood should be easy. One bite?

A long exhale shuffled out the vibrations of anger. Calm and resolute control were required. Michael would not rage. No, it wasn't necessary. He pitied this woman. He hated her. He adored her. He was twisted into all sorts by her.

Should he give her his blood, she would heal.

In essence, he would be betraying Jane.

"It's not so much to ask, is it, Michael? Your woman won't mind. She needn't even know. I require you serve me for a week or so."

"A week?" Serve her?

"It requires much blood. To bathe in it would be preferable."

"Absolutely not!" Almost, *almost* he had been in her hands again. Like a lovesick fool, a naive boy who craved the attention of a worldly woman. "You're doing it again, Isabelle. You march into my life, seduce me, take what you will, then traipse off in your diamonds and silks like a spoiled princess grown bored of her playthings."

"I wouldn't leave you if you would have me. Does she mean that much to you? Could you love me, Michael?"

He'd never seen Isabelle beg. To reduce herself to a wanting, pleading thing.

"I can't do this. Not now. I need…to think."

"But you won't rule it out?"

"Isabelle!" He swung around to put his face before her, to make her see that he struggled, that he hurt, that he was a man who did not need her. But there, so close to her, and surrounded by her seductive scent, her life, her blood and her pulse, he fell— and got lost in the memory of better times.

Michael curled his hand up the back of Isabelle's head and drew her in for a kiss. A long, deep, moaning kiss that tortured him while it fed the wanting hole he'd carried in his heart for the years following her abrupt departure.

Their heartbeats traced a furious path, pounding, pounding inside his skull. But he did not relent. The taste of her in his mouth, oh…her blood…

Realizing his teeth had come down, and that he'd cut her lip, Michael pulled away abruptly. He swiped a hand over the blood on his lower lip. Isabelle grinned.

Her blood, not his. She could have bitten him, latched on to his neck just now and taken the elixir required to heal, and yet she had not.

"I want you to give it freely," she said, sliding a finger across her mouth to clean away the blood. "That kiss was a reaction. You didn't even know you were going to do it until it happened, yes?"

"Yes." He knelt there on the floor, huffing, wanting, aching. The taste of her he tried to forget, but he would never ignore champagne poured into his mouth. "I can't do it, Isabelle. I—I love Jane."

"Jane Rénan, the daughter of a witch and a vampire."

"How do you know?"

"I've my ways."

Right. She'd put the weird video on his iPod somehow. Of course, she was following him, and those he associated with.

"So you're with the daughter of a witch? Doesn't her blood have any effect on you?"

"I've not bitten her."

Isabelle laughed. So deep and tremulous, it registered in Michael's belly, teasing him to a quick arousal. "Such restraint, Michael. How long do you think that will last? With me, you've no worry of death. My blood will feed you, make you stronger."

"I am stronger," he spat. "Much stronger than you will ever be."

Standing, Michael paced over to the door. He'd stayed long enough. If he remained, he'd be on the couch tearing that thin fabric from her breasts in order to feed the lust. "Strong enough to walk away from you. Goodbye, Isabelle."

"You said you'd think about it!"

Without a glance to the master of his creation, Michael marched outside into the sunlight. "I will," he said. "I will.

Chapter 21

How could he *not* think about the only woman he had ever loved? Sure it had been five decades earlier, but there were days, if Isabelle's image crossed his thoughts, he could feel the intense emotion they had shared as if it were new and present and real.

Isabelle LePierre, daughter of a count, born in the sixteenth century. Seductress. Lover. Vampire.

Michael had already gone through the obvious questions: Had she done this to other men? Make them love her, and then bite them and flee? Of course. Did she care? She may have once, while they were together, but not after she left. The very minute she slipped away from him, Michael suspected she had already thoughts of a new conquest in mind. Was it habitual for her to go from one man to the next? Probably, after living for so long, it had to be her way of survival. He knew addictions. She may not be aware of her sexual need, and yet, nothing could stop her from seeking that next fix.

But the troubling question was: Why him?

If Isabelle had created other blood children, then why hadn't she returned to one of them to ask for the healing blood she required? Why Michael?

And why now, when he suddenly found himself involved with a new woman, someone who could erase every memory of Isabelle LaPierre with but a smile and a flash of those sexy faery tale eyes.

He loved Jane.

But you are not bonded to her. You can never be.

Without the blood, there would always be something lacking between them. That sense of utterly being a part of the other person—just by thinking of them. Like it was with Isabelle.

Michael shrugged his hand back through his hair. He drove toward Jesse's house. And Jane. Moving away from Isabelle.

Is this what he wanted? To return to Jane. To step away from a past that had haunted him for years?

Wasn't he supposed to be in exile, getting over his addiction? Not that he was concerned about that. Hell, he may have already replaced that habit with the sex magic. And yet, women would enter and women would leave his life. The need for blood would always remain.

Thinking of which… He was hungry. It had been

days since he'd taken blood. And going home to Jane wasn't going to make anything easier. He should have stopped in town.

The Mini pulled onto a gravel road and rumbled slowly over the pot holes and loose pebbles. He could turn around, head back.

Instead, he stepped on the gas.

He'd have to deal. Somehow. So long as Jane was busy with her work, maybe he could slip inside and slink down to the basement. If he shut himself away in the coffin, sleep would come, and he could ignore the blood hunger.

But could he ignore Isabelle's plea for wholeness?

Hanging up the phone, Jane delighted at the expectation of seeing the cake she'd ordered. The baker had said it would be an interesting challenge, but nothing was impossible. It would be delivered tomorrow, on Michael's birthday.

Now, if only the rest of her life were so easy as ordering cake.

Michael breezed through the doorway and when she thought he hadn't noticed her in the kitchen, he paused and looked to her. Something wasn't right. But he smiled and tilted his head in earnest concern. "Jane. What are you up to?"

She beamed. "Nothing. I've been waiting for you."

He could sense her anxiety, she knew that; and so she wished it away. *Don't think of tomorrow night.*

Spreading her fingers across his chest, she mined

for his heartbeat and found it pounded rapidly beneath her palm. "Everything all right with you? Blood?"

He touched the small spot of red on his shirt sleeve. "My own. Truth."

"New clothes?"

He tugged down the hem of the long-sleeved tee shirt. A distorted black skull had been screen printed onto the lower left side of the gray fabric. "I find I've become an extra large." He took her hand and placed it over his groin. "So what have you been up to today? Catch up on your work?"

"Yes, I did."

He took her hands from his body, and, spinning her into a dance pose, pressed against her and swayed her around for a few steps. His light mood felt so good, she couldn't find the words to protest.

"It's good to stand in your arms, Jane. Everything is right here with you. We should go dancing tomorrow night. For my birthday. Can we do that?"

"We could put on some tunes and dance in the workroom? Make it our own private ballroom."

"Fill the room with flowers and candlelight and soft music." He dipped her masterfully. "Just you and me dancing under the moonlight."

Yes, that damned full moon. And Ravin had yet to call her back. Jane swirled out of the dip. "So, where did you go besides the stores? You've been gone the entire afternoon."

Michael leaned against the stove and bowed his head. Everything was wrong.

"Michael, what is it?"

"You know the other night when I thought I saw a face on my iPod. Well, I did, and it was a familiar face. And there was a new entry in the address book."

"What does that mean?"

"This afternoon I went to the address. The reporter from the graveyard lives there. The kid from the club that talked to you. He took me—" a heavy sigh engulfed his powerful frame in a feeble cringe "—to my blood master."

"Your what? Oh. The vampire who created you?"

"Yes. Isabelle LaPierre."

Jane uttered a tiny sound.

"I haven't seen her since the night she transformed me, fifty years ago."

"But she's sought you out? To find you here, in this small town? Michael, what does she want? Oh. I suppose it's none of my business."

"Really? You don't want to know about the afternoon I've spent with a sexy, four-hundred-year old woman?"

"Sexy?"

He shrugged a hand through his hair and sighed. "Devastatingly so."

"Oh." Jane sat on a kitchen chair and tilted her head into her hand. "What did she want? I want to know."

Michael sat on the table before her and tilted up her chin to inspect her eyes. He shouldn't do this to her, bring her into his past, but he wanted to see her reaction. As well, she needed to know everything about him if they were ever to have a future together.

"She's been burned. The complete right side of her face is scarred."

"But you said she was sexy."

"She remains so. Jane, a woman's beauty is not what a man reads on her face, but rather from within. A witch spat upon her."

"Good."

He delivered her a scathing look, fisted his fingers, but wouldn't reproach her. She had every right to her opinions. And the undertones of jealousy pleased him.

Clasping a hand over her beating heart, Jane couldn't find her voice. She wanted to speak, he could sense it, but this time her pulse was not so calm. Anger laced her scent. Delicious and thick and startling.

Can't use your magic to overcome jealousy, can you, Jane?

"Why has she contacted you?"

"Only a blood child can give her the restorative blood required to erase the scarring."

"And you gave it to her?"

"Not yet." The small taste of Isabelle's blood still lingered on his palate. It was too rich for words. Too splendid to share with anyone, even if it was only in description.

"So you'll return to her," Jane stated.

"I'm considering whether or not that would be wise."

"What if I ask you not to?"

"Would you?" Amused by her indifferent daring,

Michael studied the play of emotions on Jane's face. Confusion danced with anger, and yet a sweetness of character befuddled the wanting rise of rage.

He could take her right now, suck out her blood and fill his mouth with her essence—before it killed him.

And isn't that what he'd wished for upon first sight of her? That she plunge the knife into his heart and kill him long, slow and hard?

For then he wouldn't have to make this choice between two women. If he did choose to give Isabelle his blood, there would be a price to pay. Their blood bond would be renewed, it would become more than he could control. Jane would cease to matter. No witch magic could fulfill him as the mistress of his creation could.

"What do you want to do?" she asked.

"I need to think about it some. And I won't be dissuaded by your efforts to guilt me."

"I'm not trying to guilt you, I'm trying to…lay claim to you."

She clutched his shirt. Her fingernails dug painfully into his chest. Good pain, that, for he could still feel despite his desire not to.

"She's a part of you, as I can never be a part of you. You've shared blood. Don't think I don't understand the power of such a connection. She'll heal. Eventually. Don't do it, Michael. Be mine. Take me."

He shook his head. "Jane, I'm tired." He slipped his fingers through hers and, though he didn't tug, she followed his gentle nudge and pressed her entire body against his, tucking her head into his neck to breathe in his anxiety.

"Can we make love?" she whispered. "I missed you."

"Feels good to have someone say that to me. You make me want to be better, Jane."

"You are better, Michael. You can't prevent the need for blood. It is a part of you. And you don't need the adrenaline anymore, because you've got me. My magic."

"True." He breathed into her hair and stroked her back. "You tempt me."

"Why must I tempt? You can have me, as you wish. Now, whenever, forever."

"I haven't fed. I'm… Your blood smells so good, Jane." Michael moaned. "I won't be able to resist, not even your chains could keep me from biting into you. Please don't ask me to risk so much."

"But I am. I want you to risk it all for me, Michael. Prove to me there is no other woman you would rather be with. Make love to me. Now."

Michael pulled Jane into the studio. "We need music. It'll refocus my cravings, should they rise. Can we do it loud and hard?"

Jane's hand slipped around the front of his jeans and squeezed, not too gently, his erection. "Hard is good," she purred. "We going to do it right here in the studio? On the floor?"

Michael shoved The Fallen CD into the player. Jane ran her palms up under his shirt and raked at his chest with her nails, converting the frenetic noise into useful distraction.

"Meet me in the bedroom. I won't crank up this until you're out of ear damage range."

He watched her slink across the hallway, long, thoroughbred legs sashaying under the sexy silk skirt. No panties, praise the devil, her master.

Flicking the volume to high, he took off across the hallway.

Jane danced to a different beat. Swaying in the center of the room, at the end of the bed, her arms twisted in a sexy Spanish lure. Her head back and her eyes focused on him, she pressed a kiss to the tip of her finger and blew it his way.

Slapping the blown kiss against his heart, Michael fell to his knees. Erratic guitars and vigorous drums scurried through the house, filling the framework. The beat, born in his veins, could not capture his sweet, wild Jane. Nor did he wish it to.

Filled with Jane, her scent, her rhythm, her air, he inhaled, closing his eyes to take it all in. Sex magic. It was an amazing thing.

Spellbound, Michael remained an adoring fan, genuflecting before her, as she twisted and shimmied closer. Tiny silver coins edged the crimson skirt she wore and tinkled near her ankles. Every lilting sway of her hips tugged at him.

"All night long," he crooned, and went up on his knees as Jane's skirts dusted his cheek and she danced around behind him. "All night," he said softly.

He vowed his heart to her silently. This dancing vision of otherworldliness. A woman trapped between the normal and the glimmering exoticness of the paranormal. He worshipped her. And even if he could not speak it aloud to her, he pledged only to her. She tamed his monster. He needed no other, no wicked blood mistress to tempt him back into her arms. He could be true to Jane. He wanted to be.

If only he could resist the *need*. For even as he swayed to the music, he felt the delicious sting of his fangs against his lower lip. Not completely descended, but soon, he knew. Soon.

Jane's sensuous rhythm seeped into his heartbeats and together their pulses synched. They called to one another beyond voice, gesture or sight. It was innate.

Dancing her feet to either side of his knees, Jane settled slowly, hips rocking and that gorgeous flat stomach shimmying before his face, until she sat upon his thighs. They went down together in a tangle of kisses and tearing silk.

Yes, he tore off her shirt. What man could take the time to mess around with those delicate little straps on her shoulders? He wanted now, and he would have her. If he took her quickly, then maybe he could outrun the monster.

Jane murmured when he ran his tongue across her nipple. Her body arched into his, her hip grinding against him. Ridiculous need gushed through him.

The music had entered her, drawing her own demon out and demanding it be fed. For she pushed his head lower, and his tongue trailed over her abdomen. Sweet like flowers and some kind of forbidden fruit, her innate perfume.

And there, deep within, he could feel the rush of life as it danced through her veins, seeking the beat. Blood scent. Pure. Wicked. Like none other he'd smelled before. Perhaps steeped with the centuries of life given her by her parents; immortality, how sweet upon the tongue.

Tearing away the skirt from her hips, the silk ties defied him from completely removing it. He kissed her deeply and teased her to the edge he loved to hear her fly over. Her scent tempted the monster.

She glided a probing finger over the thick scar on his right shoulder. "What's this from? It must have been deep."

"Jesse burned me with a cross."

"What? That's awful!"

He smirked and nipped at the underside of her chin. Rising onto one fist, he slapped a palm across his arm and inspected the scar. "It was stupid, but, right after I told him I was a vamp, he demanded proof. The fangs didn't do it because Jesse had seen too many movie props. So, Jesse, obliging bastard he can be, grabbed the wood cross from his wall and pressed it to me."

"He could have done some serious damage."

"You don't think this is serious? It hurt like hell. Jesse felt awful. But he believed me. I've always had to stay away from the sacred." He tugged her skirt, but it insisted on clinging to her hips. "But you're not sacred, are you?"

"Never."

Michael captured the end of her gasp with his tongue. He flicked it inside her mouth.

She pulled him on top of her and gripped his hair, tugging gently, then harder. And when she dove off the cliff and began to fly, his teeth grazed the slim twisted silk tie of her skirt—and cut through the fabric.

Flinging back his hair to clear it from his eyes, he stretched his mouth and gnashed at the air.

Grasped by the shoulders, Michael plunged into Jane's fast breaths. She kissed him on the mouth. He tried to pull away from her. *Madness red want need.* Oh, the delicious pain of tasting her flesh with his teeth.

"Jane, no." He protested, but not very loudly.

Just one bite? A small taste? Surely, he could risk that? Would the sex magic overwhelm the death cocktail?

A sigh of surrender to the end of the orgasm, and Jane relaxed, her shoulders settling onto the hardwood floor, her fingers slipping from his shoulders.

"Kiss me again," she murmured, eyes closed, completely unaware of the monster that had just made its way into the room. Giggles, those sweet, satiated trills of joy, punctuated her final pulse of pleasure. "Please, Michael."

Twisting his head down and pressing the crown of it against her collarbone, Michael fought the rising urge. Focus. Not red. *Not red.* It was everywhere, the blood scent, filling the room and drowning out the frantic guitar solo that skidded toward destruction in lightning fast licks.

His chest heaving, and fists forming near Jane's head, Michael knew he should push away. But an even more insistent part of him wasn't about to leave.

He thought he'd begun to take control!

"Michael? Oh, no."

"I warned you I needed to feed."

Jane pressed her fingers against his lips. He had but to jerk to the left and a canine would razor through her skin. Seeming to realize the stupid move, she pulled away. Her legs scissored under his as she pushed herself across the floor.

"We can handle this, Michael. Don't let it control you."

He wasn't hearing her anymore. The music blasted. The blood hunger pulsed like sixteenth notes in his ears. Every pore on his body craved Jane. Jane in his arms. Jane wrapped around his need. Jane inside his mouth. Jane slipping down his throat.

"Jane…" he gasped. "Go!"

"No!" She twisted beneath him. Her elbow caught him against the jaw, not hard, but the cloying scent of blood permeated his pores.

Slipping out from under him, Jane gripped her elbow. She leaned forward, studying his face.

Just as Michael pushed out his tongue, she swiped the back of her hand across his lips. She looked at her elbow. A slash of crimson glistened. Which meant— There had been a stain of *her* blood on his tooth.

Michael lashed up his tongue. He tasted nothing.

"It's gone. I got it all." Panic deepened her eyes to an impossible emerald glint. "You can't do this, Michael. Do you want to die?"

"You're not a witch, Jane. You're just plain Jane." He followed her journey across the floor, again on all fours. "You can't hurt me. But I can hurt you."

"Is that what you want? To hurt me? All you need do is return to your blood master, that'll do the trick." Reaching the doorway, she scrambled up to stand. Her skirt hung loosely about her hips, the ties to fasten it hadn't come undone. Her ruby-capped breasts taunted him, her lips plump from their wicked kisses. "Listen to the music!"

Michael roared up onto his feet and lunged toward Jane. The sting of her Louisville slugger slap sent him reeling off balance. He staggered backward and landed on the bed.

Gripping his knees and hanging over, Michael tasted his own blood. The woman packed a mighty wallop. "Cripes, that was a good one."

"Yeah?" She looked at her fist, and then smiled. "Yeah."

"But not good enough," he muttered. "You want to play rough?"

"I want to play safe, Michael. No blood. Promise?"

She slid over his legs and knelt on the bed. Sweeping up her hair with her hands and then stretching out her arms, she displayed her body before him, all miles and miles of angry hair and perfect handfuls of breast and lickable stomach and thighs.

Before he could reach to grab her hair, Jane slapped a hand onto his chest, pushing him back onto the bed. "Heel, vampire. Hands above your head."

He clenched the bed frame. His teeth had not retracted. And yet, this new side of Jane coaxed up the urge to get inside her—with his body and not his teeth.

"You won't," she said. "You don't want this to end, do you?"

He nodded, agreeing.

"Now." She tugged down his jeans, and pushed them beyond his knees. Creeping back up to kiss him, she then tapped his upper lip. "Open up, I want to touch."

His teeth? Weirdly turned on, Michael opened up. Jane ground her hips across his erection. Her wet heat teased at his patience. And when she touched one of his fangs, he closed his eyes to keep from seeing her curious grin. Abbreviated breaths wracked his chest. So close to losing it again, he strove for control.

"Good vampire," she cooed. "They're so hard and white and sharp."

Don't cut yourself, Jane. Why was she being so cavalier about the death cocktail thing? Just moments ago he had been aching to risk it, and yet— now *she* turned the tables?

"I can't," he forced out and closed his mouth.

It was the magic; it had emboldened her.

"You can." She then lowered herself onto his hard shaft. "Take it all, Michael. *Mon Dieu,* I believe you *have* grown."

Good to know, and a fine remedy to the slap she'd delivered him. Michael pumped his hips hard against Jane's body. Each thrust moved him deeper into oblivion. Tight around him. Coming soon...

"Oh, Jane..." No monster could barge in this time. Not with Jane in control.

But the danger remained, for his fangs cut the air as he stretched his mouth to moan in bliss. The idea that they could never truly be safe with one another excited him like no chains and manacles ever could.

As Jane's fingernails dug into the flesh on his shoulders, Michael came hard and forcefully.

After slipping away to gaze at the full moon, Jane fell asleep on the chair Michael had hauled out to the cement patio. Rosy sunlight prompted her to a stretch. Sweet dew twinkled on the grass tops. An ant crept across her belly. The tickle of its small appendages made her smile dreamily. Yet, she flicked it away and scanned the ground for more of its kind. No swarm. Best not to become complacent, or relive another strange insect love-fest.

Tilting her head, Jane studied the cherub fountain that had, yet again, stopped dribbling water. Twisting her mouth in perusal, she then decided the water should run freely.

Nothing.

And then a sputter, and finally a stream.

Quietly delighted, Jane looked forward to calling her mother and telling her about this. She'd never believe it. And yet, perhaps she would. Certainly, her father could no longer hold anything against the idiot vampire.

Could Michael ever hope to tame the monster? He just needed control—a control she'd taken from him last night. Yet he'd not bitten her, much as she knew he had wanted to.

And though she'd had to use aggression to still the monster, even that had sent a rush through her. The forbidden danger of them engaging in sex, unprotected but for their frenzy, had excited her. Her inner wildness had been awakened. And she didn't want to go back to plain Jane.

Plain Jane feared the ritual. Wild Jane wanted all life could offer, no matter that she must steal it during sex. Wild Jane was a witch. Truly. And she mustn't deny her fate. She'd stepped into this mistake, knowing well what it could bring. Adventure. Excitement. Danger. Choices.

She must see it to the end.

"I wonder if it will remain?" she said of her newly emerged magic. "Or if I'll need Michael to for ever make it so?"

It would be a poor consolation should she require the man to keep up her magic. Not that she didn't enjoy making love to him, but she never wanted to depend on a man. For anything.

Scanning the sky, the sun emerging on the horizon, Jane figured about eighteen hours until midnight. The moon would be full and white. This night she must answer the call to immortality or forsake her own life.

How will you love him? If you do not exist?

Her father had a point. Was she willing to die for Michael? To never know him again?

"I love him. I can't leave this world."

But how to do it without losing Michael in the process?

Wait. Michael had found another vampire.

Sitting upright, Jane nodded. Why hadn't she considered this earlier?

She'd call her father—and Ravin—and make arrangements.

"No, you can't," she muttered. "He cares about her. It would be so wrong to let jealousy get in the way. Oh, what to do?"

The fact that there wasn't a phone in the house may just be karma trying to tell her something.

Chapter 22

The new jeans fit him snugly. Especially across the crotch.

Jane had done this to him. Increased his strength. Calmed his monster.

So why was he considering going to Isabelle?

Because she had been hurt. She didn't deserve to suffer.

She does not suffer, Michael's conscience argued, *only her ego has taken a bruising.* But what was a week of sacrificing his blood in the greater scheme of things?

Everything.

"Not today," he muttered. "I'll deal with this tomorrow."

Michael wasn't going to let anything get him down today. Today was his birthday. The parties, the presents, the...well, what would it be this year?

He didn't have a family, no mother to bake him a cake and throw him a party. The only thing close to being family, the band, was likely taking it easy right now, not even giving him a thought. As for presents, well there wasn't anything he couldn't buy for himself now.

But he still liked the idea of being surprised.

He stood in the doorway to the backyard, legs crossed and right shoulder pressed against the frame. He had yet to see Jane since rising an hour ago. Though he respected her closed workroom door. "Did she forget?"

Or had he done something again to scare her off, seeking shelter in her work? They had gotten pretty violent with each other last night.

An aching agony burst inside his throat. Jane was all he had. His only hope for some semblance of *real* family. Isabelle offered nothing but sensational adventure and a constant source of blood.

A source he couldn't overlook. If he chose Isabelle, no longer would he have to take from mortals. His risk for murder would be reduced to nil.

Hmm...

Could Jane offer him that? Sure, the strength was great. He feared no monster, or even a vigilante witch (so long as she kept her blood to herself). And the sex magic was awesome. Soaring inside of Jane was like flying.

He'd done it, hadn't he? He'd fallen hard for the woman.

What kind of fool had he become? Why couldn't he resist her?

Was the vampire attracted to the magic inside Jane? Would he need to continue to have sex with her in order to keep the power he'd gained?

What a cruel attraction, that he should crave the one woman who could prove most deadly to him?

And what was he to her? He presented no danger to Jane. A little bite could easily heal. He increased her magic. She had no risks to be involved with him.

A relationship would not be easy. The very nature of the rock 'n' roll lifestyle challenged most normal couples. Add to that the fact they were blood enemies?

To his right a crowd of crickets chirped at the night. The sun hadn't quite set, yet the moon was visible above the oak tree that mastered the back of the yard.

The moon. It made a fine birthday present. If only he could share it, so wide and round and luminous. So far from heaven.

He wondered if he had ever had a chance at heaven before he had become a vampire. Probably. Michael Lynsay, pre-vamp, had led a fairly responsible life. He'd held a job as a DJ at a radio station, and had taught music lessons after hours. He'd had goals, pastimes, and dreams. He'd even gone to church—until his mother had died.

And he'd been baptized, which now proved his very bane, for he could not look upon the sacred or touch it.

Michael stroked the soft pink flesh where he'd been burned by Banks's cross. Completely healed. Yeah, it was too late. Vampires couldn't go to heaven.

Was the sacrifice worth it?

He'd grown up hoping some day he'd become a famous singer. His mother had indulged his desires, spending a fortune on voice lessons and entering him in local singing contests. You're a natural, his voice teacher had often said. You'll go far, Michael.

And he had. But what would he do in a few decades? He couldn't take the stage forever. Someone would notice he never aged. That would be creepy, not to mention, stupid.

How would he fulfill his life? Would he have someone to stand at his side, to hold his hand, for centuries?

Like Jane's parents.

By rights, Jane should be long gone. To put up with his antics took a strong woman. And yet, there must be something about him that she liked.

She gets magic out of the deal, vampire. Don't fool yourself. She benefits greatly from this relationship.

Just a week of you serving me.

"No, it's not worth it. Isabelle will heal. She's not like my Jane," he said, and smiled. But the smile didn't last.

Where was she?

Wandering back inside, Michael lingered in the kitchen. There, on the center of the table, is where his mother had always placed a homemade chocolate cake with blue candles. He liked blue candles. Now the only soul who could ever know that was dead.

"Jane, Jane, Ja-ee-ane," he sang under his breath as he neared the studio.

The smell of flame alerted him. And…flowers?

Doing a sharp right turn, Michael strode into the workroom. Stepping abruptly backward, he slid his fingers over the doorframe.

The entire room glittered with candle flame. Thick white and blue candles were placed everywhere, along the floor before the windows, on the worktable, and in every corner. Red rose petals carpeted the floor. Like a ballroom out of some fantasy story the women cried over at the movies.

And in the midst of it all, the belle of the ball stood holding something before her. A long simple red dress skimmed her curves and fell to the floor. Soft material, Michael knew, because it jealously clung to her breasts and hips. Copper-stained hair, full and thick, sifted across her face but didn't hide those deep dark eyes. Smiling at him. Her entire body smiled. The faery tale had become reality.

"Happy birthday, rock star," she said.

"I thought you'd forgotten." He stepped across the room, careful to avoid a candle placed in his path. The urge to count the candles overwhelmed him, and he started tallying.

"Oh, no. Focus! Michael!"

"Huh?" The candles could wait. Maybe. There were half a dozen on the table, and over there—

"Michael."

"Right. I'll count later." Redirecting his focus, he centered on her heartbeats. And he didn't feel like counting those, it just felt good to know they were there, inside him. *But could they ever become completely his? Like Isabelle's heartbeats?*

Unsettled, Michael looked about. "Jane, you did this for me? What the—?"

He looked over the small cake she held on her palms. It bore no candles, and didn't say anything, but it was— "Black?"

"With glitter. I thought it would look sort of rock 'n' roll."

"Well, it certainly looks like something." Something gothic and very, very strange.

Laughter shook Michael's frame. It felt good. Damn good. He took the cake from her. Setting it aside on the table, he then spun her into his arms and did a whirl on the dance—er, workroom floor.

"Do you like it?"

"It's perfect," he said. "I feel like some kind of prince."

"Can I be your princess?"

"How about my queen? My dark queen. You look the devil's little sister in this dress." He kissed her quickly and darted a look downward. "Ja-ee-ane, I can see everything when I look down the front."

"Then look some more."

"Oh, I will. Damn, you are delicious."

"Probably not as tasty as the cake."

"Screw the cake, this is what I want to eat for my

birthday." He nipped her collarbone and followed with a lick at her chin. "And all those rose petals… how many do you think there are?"

Jane jerked him back into her eyesight. "You want to count something? Try years. How old are you, birthday boy?"

"You tell me how old you are, and I'll spill the beans."

"I've given you a clue. Besides, a woman never reveals her age, nor does a gentleman ask."

"I've never claimed to be a gentleman." And in proof he drew a wet trail with his tongue up from her breasts to under her throat.

"You're a cad. Mmm, but I wouldn't have you any other way."

"So the lady admits to liking her boys bad?"

"And wild. You said you wanted to dance with me, so let's dance. I brought in some music from the car."

"You actually listen to music?"

"Yes, I listen to music." She switched on the CD player. "Though you may not approve. It's Niyaz."

"I've heard of them. Indian fusion sort of stuff?"

"Persian."

A mixture of Turkish stringed instruments and a haunting female voice permeated the room, and Michael decided it was cool. "Doesn't matter what's playing, so long as I've got my girl in my arms."

He spun her out and the two did a few more spins before magnetically connecting to one another and then the only option was a slow sway.

Want surfaced, but riding the tease would prove immensely more satisfying than taking her right now. This night was meant to be seduced to infinity.

Over the top of Jane's head Michael looked to the darkening sky and could pick out a few twinkling stars. He held his woman in his arms. A black birthday cake sat nearby. The world glittered below him. What more could a vampire ask for?

"How much?" Baptiste watched as the witch deposited the bound body into the trunk of his rental car.

She turned and sneered. The steel studs on her leather wristbands looked sharp, and oh, so painful. "Too much for you, vampire."

"I refuse to take charity."

"Oh, yeah?" She slammed the trunk shut. "Then let me offer you a taste of my blood. It's not charity, I promise. Think of it as a gift."

He recoiled violently.

"Chill, old man." Ravin brushed her palms against each other, cleaning off traces of blood. "This is for your daughter. You're just lucky I like Jane, or you'd be ash right now."

"I believe it," he murmured. "Thank you. I owe you, Ms. Crosse."

"No, you don't. In fact, leave town as quickly as you came, or I might forget who you're related to."

"Deal."

"Could you dance with me forever, Jane?"

"Mmm." She snuggled against his chest, relaxed

in his arms. Everything between them had synched, their movements, their breaths, even their heartbeats. "No question about that."

"Think about it," he whispered. Eyes closed, he nuzzled into her freesia-scented hair. The world had slipped away. He had taken flight. "Forever. With me. Loving, living, singing, laughing. Could you do it?"

"I don't know what you're trying to say, Michael." He didn't like it when she pulled her warmth away from him. "Want some cake?"

"I don't do cake, you know that. I just…*I* could imagine it. The two of us, forever. Don't worry, I'm not asking for a commitment. I just want you to know, I could be true to you."

"Oh, Michael." She stroked his hair, swishing it over the top of his ear. "Forever is a very long time. And very much a commitment."

"Your mom and dad have done it."

"Let's just dance, Michael." She twisted her fingers into the ends of his hair and refit her body against his frame. "Hold me."

She fit him perfectly. Not once in Michael's life had he ever felt as though he required protection, or the quiet strength of a woman's presence. But Jane made him know that it was okay to have it.

This birthday was the best. He may even eat some cake, just to prove he appreciated her efforts.

"I could do it for a while," she suddenly offered. "But don't ask me to commit to forever. My forever may be entirely different from your forever."

"You said you were immortal. What makes us different?"

"I have to renew that immortality. You, well, you've a very long time to walk this earth."

Immortality renewal? Right. Something about when the great Protection had been cast to make all witches blood poison to vampire, and in turn, the witches had sacrificed their immortality. So they had a way to get it back?

"You will renew it, yes?" He leaned back, seeking the gaze she kept elusive. Could he invade her faery tale? She was afraid, he could feel it coursing through his veins. Afraid to live forever? "Jane, aren't I worth living for?"

"Of course you are. But am I worth the risk?"

She drew away from him in a fluid, but decisive move. Brushing back her hair, she glanced around and let out a heavy sigh. The candles had begun to drip down their sides and streams of blue and white wax trickled across the floor.

"You are always worth the risk, Jane. I'd risk my life for you." Not about to let her off so easily, Michael tilted up her chin. "It's my birthday, so I get to make one wish."

She shrugged. "If you believe in wishes."

"Jane, my wish is that you will renew your immortality—whatever it takes—so, no matter what happens between us, I'll always know you're around. Here for me. Even if you only want to be friends."

"You could suffice with something so minimal as mere friendship?"

"I wouldn't like it. But I understand your reluctance to commit to a guy, hell, a vampire, for so long. But you'll always be the only one for me, Jane. Believe me. You live inside of me."

He pressed his fingers over his heart. Not a stage maneuver designed to draw maximum adulation from the females. Never before had he been so sincere.

"You're the first woman I haven't drank blood from, and yet, I feel this immense connection to. Jane, I just need you."

He hugged her, and she submitted, not an ounce of reluctance in her bones. A good thing, for Michael knew she yet struggled with all that he had just offered. He'd meant it, and he'd walk the world for her to prove it.

And that felt rapturous to him.

"Jane?"

Dredged up from their embrace by the sound of a man's voice, Michael turned, Jane still close and tight in his arms. Baptiste Rénan stood in the doorway. Hadn't that man left town?

"We're celebrating," Michael said.

"An hour, Jane," Baptiste said, and left.

"An hour until what?" Michael asked. He tried to catch Jane's eyes, but she'd found a nook on his shoulder and had laid claim to the post. "What's your dad doing here?"

"Nothing to worry about. Probably he wants to say goodbye."

"I thought he left once already."

"We should have some cake," she suggested. "Even if you just lick the frosting."

"Is it chocolate?"

"It is." Jane blew away strands of hair from her lashes. "I'll run down and get some plates."

As weird as the moment had become, Michael couldn't help but think it was only going to get weirder. "What's up, Jane?"

"What do you mean? Aren't you having a wonderful time?"

"I was. But your father put a sour taste in my mouth. Is he in the house?"

"Probably outside. I told him to give us some privacy tonight."

So she knew he would be hanging around.

"I feel strange doing this, knowing he's sitting around waiting to say goodbye to you. Why don't you invite him in—"

"Michael, really, it's not a problem. I'll be right back."

She swept out of the room so quickly, three or four candles were extinguished in her wake.

Standing in the spiraling smoke of the executed candles, Michael, head bowed, struggled with the eerie tingle screeching up and down the back of his neck.

Something wasn't right. He could taste it.

Relax, man. Enjoy your birthday. It's nothing that her father is here. He *is* her father.

Striding over to the windows, cautious not to knock over the finished pieces, he searched the grounds below, but couldn't see a thing, for there were no yard lights. And yet, a glimmer in the distance caught his eye. Way back there, at the end of the vast overgrown garden. Looked like a blazing fire.

Were the neighbors burning something? He hadn't remarked any other houses close enough to consider neighbors.

"Plates and forks," Jane sang as she breezed back into the room. "I got chocolate with cherry icing in the center. I'm hoping it's your favorite."

"Of course it is," Michael said absently. He tilted his head, his focus on the flames eating into the sky beyond the yard. "Is someone out back?"

"I told you my father is out there. He's—Michael come and eat some cake."

"I am not interested any more." He strode across the room. Celebration wouldn't happen until he got to the bottom of this. "I think it's time we invited your father to the party."

Jane scrambled for him so quickly, she slid on a puddle of liquid wax and had to catch herself by grabbing Michael's arm. "Leave him by himself. He wants to be alone. Michael, please."

Searching her dark eyes Michael found something he had only once before seen in them.

"You're lying to me, Jane." He felt as incredulous as his voice had sounded. "I can feel it in the subtle tremor of your touch. And I can see it in your eyes. Fear."

Bowing her head, she prodded the edge of a wax spill with her bare toe.

"You've never lied to me. It's something about your father, isn't it? This has to do with that argument the two of you had the other night, and then you avoided me for a whole day. Talk to me. I'm not letting you go until you tell me what the hell is going on."

"Michael, please, you're being paranoid."

"Oh? Then why does your father have a bonfire lit at the end of the garden? What's he doing? Dancing up demons? Speaking a spell?"

"Don't be silly, only my mother can do that, and Daddy would never dream to attempt the sort without bringing her wrath upon him."

"Yet now, you can do the same. You're going out there in an hour to meet him. For what? A midnight fire dance? Spells and charms chanted to the moon? Tell me. I won't be angry if you want to practice your magic. But your silence—it makes me feel this is not right. If you don't tell me, I'm heading out there now."

"You can't, Michael."

He shoved her away and stalked out into the hallway. Jane's calm had fallen away and a startling fear mastered her heartbeats. He didn't want to walk away from her, but if she wasn't going to be truthful with him…

"He's prepared the ritual!" Jane called.

Michael stopped dead in the center of the hallway. Hooking his thumbs in his front pockets, he turned and asked, "Ritual?"

"To immortality," she said. Her hands swept down the front of the silk dress, and fluttered at her sides as if unsure where exactly to go, what to do. "My parents decided I should perform the immortality ritual a century ago on my twenty-fifth birthday. They wanted to ensure their daughter lived as long as they did. The ritual requires a renewal every century—as it does for all witches. Tonight is that night. The ritual must be completed before midnight."

Michael approached. His feet felt heavy, but no heavier than his heartbeats. This was not going to be good. He felt it to his very bones, so much so, his canines ached and lowered in his mouth.

"Nothing wrong with immortality," he offered.

"You did wish I would do whatever necessary to remain so."

"I agree, you should renew it. I want you to." Stopping three paces from the willowy figure who seemed to stand alone in the house, he planted his stance. "So what's the deal? Why didn't you simply tell me about this?"

"The ritual is sacred."

He shrugged, but inwardly, he shivered at that word—sacred.

"Also—" she fretted, clasping her hands together, then as quickly splaying them furiously before her "—the ritual requires I consume the blood from a vampire's beating heart."

Chapter 23

Pressing his palm out before him as a feeble blockade against the awful words he'd heard come from Jane's mouth, Michael felt his entire body wince. "A vampire's beating heart?"

To her credit Jane didn't rush out an explanation.

"You—" he delivered the weighted words carefully "—you…are immortal…because you drank the blood from a—a vampire's beating heart?"

"A century ago," she said, as if explaining something so mundane as her choice of red as opposed to pink for her dress.

"And now you have to do it again."

He wouldn't release her gaze. If he could hold her with his eyes, then time stopped, and everything that didn't make sense ceased to matter anyway. The faery tale would remain just that, a tale, not truth.

But he couldn't help himself. "A heart? From a vampire. Still…be—"

She made a move toward him but he stopped her by fisting his fingers.

This woman had calmly confessed to something so insane.

"Jane, did you hear yourself? You said—What the hell is your dad doing out there? Is he—and me?"

The pieces fell together rapidly. Michael turned and marched away from her.

"Michael, stop! You can't go out there!"

"Why not? Or do you have some ritual to carry me out there? I'm your sacrifice? You going to rip out my heart and eat it?"

"I would never dream to hurt you."

"Oh, really? Where you going to find another vampire on such short notice?"

"My father has a contact. You met my friend Ravin."

"Friend? You have friends who will supply you with live vampires so you can rip out their hearts and have a snack? Wait—she was checking me out, wasn't she? Did the two of you plan this? To get me, and then to—"

He raced down the stairs and ran out into the backyard. A bonfire spat into the sky and lit the entire end of the garden. He couldn't make out figures, but Baptiste had to be down there somewhere.

This was nuts. All this time, had he been a part of Jane's quest to remain immortal?

The witch—Ravin Crosse—she'd been there when he'd arrived in the graveyard. She had been stalking him more than Isabelle had!

"Stop right there and hear me out, Michael."

Spinning on his heels, he smiled at her gall. The sweet, innocent earth mother reveals her wicked side. She really was the devil's sister.

Raging up to her, he pressed her against the wall of the house, hands high over her head and pinning her wrists. "You weren't going to tell me about this, were you? Were you!"

"It's your birthday, I didn't want to spoil—"

"Oh, you've ruined the fun, Jane. And now that you have, give me one good reason why I should let you go through with this."

"It's not your place to say whether I can or cannot do a thing."

She pushed away from him and stomped into the center of the yard. Fury designed her hair in a wild rage about her face, and the red dress seemed so out of place. So elegant. Bloodred. So bloody red.

"I understand now. You've been stringing me along since the beginning. Tap into the vampire's sex magic and when you're finished with him, then crack open his heart."

Michael kicked the wall. Then again and again. He was mad about her. Mad in love. How could he love someone so much?

And now to hear this? How could he have been so foolish?

Jane remained in his direct path to running to

the back of the garden. "You're more bloodthirsty than I am!"

"Oh, and on what high moral ground you walk, Mr. Fallen Angel? Look at you! Raging over *my* little indiscretion?"

"Little? Woman!"

"How dare you judge me? You, who drinks blood every day—and not because you need to but because you *want* to. Don't you dare throw stones at me!"

She had a strange point. Why was he raging?

Because Jane did not stand before him. She had changed, without asking him if it was all right. She was *his*. Her heartbeats pulsed in his veins. And he'd almost had his finger on the control button. Things had been *that close* to being right.

And she wanted to rip out his heart.

"I can't look at you right now." He kicked in the back door to the garage and wandered inside, seeking the solace of the cool empty shadows. Anger coursing through his veins, he slammed his fist into the cement wall. The flesh cracked and blood drooled out.

"You said you wanted me to do this!" she called from outside. "Well, now you've got your birthday wish."

Pressing his face to the wall, Michael opened his mouth wide in a silent scream. It felt as though she'd reached in and ripped out his heart, and held it dripping and bloody before him for his inspection— before she bit into it.

He *had* told her he'd wanted her to live forever. For him. Selfish bastard.

And now that she was going ahead with it, who was he to stop her?

Jane ran barefoot through the tangled sumac that twisted upon the ground and up and around the stalks of the shrubbery. It tripped her up a few times, but she persisted, keeping one eye to the back of the house.

She hadn't wanted it to come out this way. Plans to lure him away to a concert for the evening had been trashed once she'd learned about his birthday. Michael had forced her hand. Yet, had she truly believed she could have kept it a secret from him?

She landed on the open grounds out back of the garden. Twigs and dead leaves crunched under her bare feet. A bonfire blazed madly. Heavy smoke-infused air filled her lungs. He hadn't followed her.

There was no time for mistakes, or to pause.

Spying the vampire roped to the tree stopped her cold. Jane stifled a scream at the sight of her. Her arms were wrenched around and behind the trunk and her ankles secured with more rope. Dressed in a pale cream suit, she looked so elegantly tattered and—

"A female?"

It struck at her heart, the callous disregard for another living, breathing *woman* that Jane swallowed back her bile. She hadn't expected it to be a woman. Of course, there were female vampires, but... She'd thought it would be a man. And so petite and beautiful?

Her head hung before her, long white hair streaming down the front of the cream jacket. She'd been knocked out, but Jane trusted her father had not bitten her. The source must not be tainted.

A female. Could she do this? To another woman?

Baptiste appeared as Jane strode around the fire. "It's time, dearest."

"Why did you bring a woman?"

"I hadn't known you favored one sex or the other."

"It's not that, I just, well— Yes, it is. I don't feel right doing this. Who is she?"

"Just a vampire, darling. Ms. Crosse plucked her for me. Female or male, it matters not to the final result. Does it trouble you that much?"

Twisting her gaze from the helpless vampire, Jane shook her head. Determination stirred her to vigorously rub her arms with her palms. "No. I'm fine. I can do this. I must do this."

Nodding, Jane bent as her father placed an amulet around her neck. A harlequin quartz crystal suspended on a chain of solid platinum. A strand of tiny red diamonds ran through the center of the stone. It belonged to her mother. Roxane had earned it on the eve of her ascension.

Jane clasped the quartz, diverting her frenzied thoughts from the awfulness of imminent destruction to the solid piece. "Ravin didn't come?"

"We made the exchange in town," her father said. "I didn't want to spend a moment longer with the witch than necessary. You understand."

Yes, the only witch her father trusted was his

wife. What would he do when he discovered Jane had come into her magic through a vampire, who had in turn taken the magic from her? No time to discuss it.

"There's no time to waste, Daddy. Michael found out."

"Where is he?"

"Back at the house. Let's do this! Before he gets the nerve to try and stop me. I don't remember the incantation. Oh, it's been so long!"

Her father drew her into a hug. Though fear and anxiety dueled with determination his embrace calmed it all. "Don't panic. It'll be fine."

Kisses to the crown of her head stilled her, brought her back to a place where all was right and nothing bad could ever happen to her. She felt him slide a piece of paper into her hand. "Mustn't be nervous. This is you, Jane. Your life."

A life chosen by her parents. Had she asked for immortality? Never.

And yet, should she not perform the ritual, she would cease to exist, to never again see her mother or father. *Or Michael.*

Now that she had her magic, there was so much to learn. A whole new world waited for her discovery.

She was not the same woman she'd been when she'd first arrived at the mansion. She'd changed. This woman who had raced toward the fire was her very core, the wild yet controlled woman who had emerged the other night after taming the vampire's sexual beast. There was no doubt, she must perform the ritual. Yes, this *is* her life.

"Do this, and you will live to love that vampire," Baptiste said. "I pray he will not harm you for your sacrifice."

"And what if I harm him? I'm the dangerous one in this relationship. One drop of my blood, and Michael…" Her breaths ached at the back of her throat.

A wistful glance toward the back of the house did not spy Michael. He hated her now. She'd played this wrong. So much she could not control. But it was too late to make amends. Too late to walk away—and she would not.

"What is this?" She opened the paper he'd handed her and immediately recognized the handwriting.

"Mother sent that along. She suspected you would not remember the incantation. I like the pink ink, don't you?"

Jane smirked. Her mother dotted her i's with perfect circles. Like a note passed to a friend during a boring class. Yet, this note would seal Jane's fate. A very bloody fate.

Turning to the vampire, she saw she was not conscious. Firelight glimmered upon her pale hair like jewels embedded in white sand, and an elegant, close-cut suit didn't show a wrinkle. "Have you harmed her?"

"Not at all. Didn't even bite the sassy bit. But I had to knock her out. She struggled so against the binds. Put pretty little cuts about her wrists. Very·tempting, I must say. Hurry then, Jane. The moon is high."

Sliding her fingers over the paper, she began to read the writing. It was difficult to see in the darkness and with the blaze behind her, so she adjusted her position, but knew she must remain close to the sacrifice.

The first words would claim her right to the incantation through her forbearers through her mother's line. "I am of Desrues blood and forged of love and magic. Guarded by the great Protection. I am as all others. Receive my call for life everlasting."

Falling onto her knees below the tree where the vampire had been tied, Jane cried out her plea to the moon to grant her immortality. A boon that was once sacrificed by an entire nation of witches in order to bespell their blood poisonous to the vampires. The words put an ancient rhythm into the ether, opening Jane to receive the blessing. The gift of vampire's blood would fortify the sacrifice.

Stretching her arms out wide, Jane called to her father. "I am ready!"

She did not watch. The crunch of her father's footsteps over the grass and fallen twigs told her he approached the tree. With a pick ax. The vampire's chest must be cleaved open, the heart torn out, and the blood consumed while it yet pulsed with life.

Her father heaved. He swung the ax.

"Jane, no!"

She opened her eyes.

The ax glinted with amber firelight. Michael ran up from behind the tree. He didn't see Baptiste. Nor did Jane's father seem to notice him.

Chapter 24

"She can't do this alone. She is a part of me. I can feel her in my veins. She has given me so much. Jane!"

Michael kicked open the garage door and ran outside. At the end of the garden, the bonfire blazed wildly. He skirted the hedges and ran down the limestone path. The lilac bushes blocked his strides, but he slapped them out of the way.

He could see figures moving before the fire, shadowed like demons stalking the flame. Two of them? Her father must be helping her.

"Not without me."

Jane had accepted him without question. She had loved him, and had even encouraged him to fight the addiction that could have pushed him to commit murder. And had she ever asked for anything in return?

That she could now finally control the magic had been a surprise to both of them.

He had done nothing but take from her. Now it was time to give back.

"Jane!"

Michael reached the oak tree. Massive in size, it blocked the view of the figures. He couldn't see the fire until he swung around the wide trunk. And he also saw a glint of steel. In a split second he registered it as a weapon—swinging toward his heart.

Spurred to defense, he slapped his hands to the curved blade scything the air. Connection stung his palms but the cutting end remained safely out of play. The momentum of the swing moved into Michael's arms, and he had no choice but to follow the direction.

Blade gripped fiercely, he teetered to the left, and brought the one who had swung the ax down with him.

A female scream scurried through the sky, but the bonfire muted it with its own roar.

Michael rolled over Baptiste, who would not release the ax. "What the hell?" He managed to twist the wooden handle from the vampire's weak grip and pressed the pick ax across his chest effectively pinning him. "You could have killed me!"

"You shouldn't have rushed in—" Baptiste huffed. Michael gave the ax a shove and the elder vampire winced "—without looking. The ceremony! Jane hasn't time for your nonsense. She needs to do this now!"

Much as Baptiste struggled, Michael was stronger. Thanks to having sex with his daughter. Hadn't this old vampire gotten strength from his wife, the witch?

With a grunt, Michael tugged the ax from Baptiste's grip, and pushed up to stand. Jane stood before the fire, hands clasped in a tight clutch before her mouth. Utter horror consumed the faery tales in her eyes.

Preparing to whip the ax into the air, Michael swung around behind him, and just before he let go of the handle, he saw the tree. And the person bound by arms, ankles and neck to the massive trunk.

"No." He abruptly stopped the momentum of his swing, the ax still in hand. "You were going to kill her?" The word *kill* choked out as he gasped back a surprising rush of emotion. Rage crushed through anguish, and echoed out in a scream. "Isabelle!"

"Michael!" Jane rushed up to him. Wild hair billowed out like flame dancing a triumphant reel. Her embrace about his shoulders didn't feel right. Too possessive. She had betrayed him.

She intended to sacrifice his blood master?

He shrugged Jane off and turned to look at her. Finding her gaze in the fire-flickered darkness required him twisting her chin up to look into his eyes straight on. Touching her felt vile. Her breath on his hand burned like the sacred. "Do you hate me that much?" he asked.

"What?"

He thrust a gesture over his shoulder. "Isabelle.

Why her? Of all the vampires in this world, you had to choose the one I would care to lose?"

"I didn't—"

He shook her by the shoulders, not finding the proper remorse in her eyes. Seeing only the flames dancing there, and wanting to wrest her about and bind her to the tree so she could know the horror.

"I didn't know it was her!"

"Liar! And I came back here to help you."

"Help? Michael, there is nothing you can do."

"Release her!" he growled.

Jane flinched. He'd yelled right into her face. But she wasted no time in responding. "Daddy, do it!"

Baptiste remained standing behind his daughter, arms crossed high upon his chest.

"That's your blood master? I had no idea, Michael. I—I didn't know they were going to bring her." Reflected flames glittered in Jane's tears as they streamed down her cheeks. "You have to believe me, Michael. I would never do anything to hurt you. Or someone you love!"

He ground his jaw tightly. She lied. She needed a vampire's heart, the bloodthirsty witch. She would say anything to get it.

Maybe.

How convenient the timing of this ritual, that it had coincided with Jane getting full use of her magic. He had played into this game so blindly!

Swinging the ax, it soared through the air, wrenching Michael's shoulders and body around. The ax connected with the oak tree. The thick white rope split, releasing Isabelle's feet. Another swing cut through the bindings about her neck, and finally, she dropped.

Plunging to catch her before her limp body hit the ground, Michael slipped his free arm under her chest and knelt at the base of the trunk, cradling her body to him.

Seductive even now, her exotic perfume crept into him and coaxed her heartbeats to follow. So slow, her pulse, but strong yet. He prayed they had not done anything like drug her.

"What did you do to her?"

"Nothing," Jane answered. "Daddy brought her while we were inside dancing."

Michael winced to know he'd been spinning about with Jane while this had been happening to Isabelle. Shouldn't he have known she was close? Felt her?

You had only eyes for the witch.

He glared at Baptiste, who stood before Jane, protecting with a forceful stance. His sneer revealed a glint of fang. "My daughter speaks the truth. I was the one who found Isabelle LaPierre, and thanks to the vigilante witch, we captured her easily. Jane had no idea the source would be your blood master. She protested, but there was no time. It is almost midnight! Will you sacrifice Jane so that bitch may live?"

Not a bitch. But when had he ever truly known this woman?

Michael hugged Isabelle's lithe body to him. She stirred. Her fingers clutched for his shirt. Her tiny moan cut right into his heart. Pulse beats moved slowly through him, warning, but unable to fully return to a normal pace.

"Have you drugged her?"

"I have no idea what the witch did to coerce her," Baptiste said.

Which meant that yes, she had been drugged.

"It is one or the other," Baptiste demanded. "You cannot keep them both."

"Daddy, don't say that. It is not Michael's choice to make." Jane stood backlighted by the great fire, arms wrapped across her chest, shivering. The red dress was sheer, shadowing her limbs in sensual play of darkness and glowing crimson. "I should have never attempted this. I didn't want to harm her. Please, Michael, take her and leave."

"Jane, you've but moments!" Her father raged now, dismissing his calm demeanor with a stomp. "Do not sacrifice yourself for a fleeting love affair!"

Michael set Isabelle upon the ground and placed the ax handle in her delicate fingers. Still groggy, she curled her fingers about it, and looked to him, her eyelids fluttering. Yes, fighting some drug—and a powerful one at that. There could be no other reason for her languishing strength.

He smoothed the hair from her lashes and traced the scars at the side of her temple. She nodded once, and closed her eyes to settle against the tree stump.

Breathing in through his nose, Michael drew in one more whiff of Isabelle. A survivor, this woman, merely going through life in pursuit of the addiction that demanded it be fed. If he had given her what she asked, he could have prevented this horrible moment.

But who can know what goes on in the minds of others?

He would know. Now.

Michael stood and approached Jane. She took a step back, but her father did not move, and so she stopped.

"Is he right?" Michael asked, the venom of his anger stabbing out in his tone. "Is it fleeting?"

Trembles shook Jane's entire body. "Never. I love you, Michael. I always will."

"Yet, you would harm someone who gave me this life?"

She shook her head. "Absolutely not. There is no question that you should take her and leave. Now."

Seeming to form her thoughts as she spoke, she avoided his gaze, instead flashing her eyes from the ground, over to the tree, and back to the ground between them. "It was good we had a chance to know one another," she offered. "I'll miss you."

"Jane, no!" Baptiste raged. "My daughter will not die because of you, vampire!"

"Daddy! It is done."

"You're not going anywhere, Jane." Michael stepped back, then turned and stalked over to the tree. He grabbed the ax. One final stroke of his finger across Isabelle's cheek, the angry flesh like crumpled silk. He swallowed back the regret. She truly was a survivor. And if she would not forgive him for what he wished to do, then he could live with that.

Resolute, he knew what had to be done. He'd come back here for one reason. And that reason remained.

"Stand back, Baptiste!" Marching back to Jane, he growled and flashed his fangs as Baptiste made to step before his daughter. "Away!" he commanded the old vampire.

"Do it," Jane hissed to her father. "Please."

Slowly, Baptiste lifted his hands before him and stepped back. Two paces. No more. Michael did not blame him for wanting to stay close. The need to protect Jane hummed in the air. Though it was ironic—she could actually cause him the most harm.

He shoved the ax into Jane's hands. "Take me."

"What?"

"Do as I say. I was being selfish up at the house," Michael said. "This is something you need. Or you will die. I don't want that. I love you, Jane." He twisted his grip on the ax handle, their clenched fists touching. "I came back here to offer my heart to you. Emotionally, and…physically."

"No!"

"Jane," her father cautioned.

"Michael, I will do no such thing! What reason would I have to live—for ever—without you?"

Tears burst anew from her eyes, raining upon Michael's wrists. He could smell her pain, and feel it in the erratic race of her pulse. He could feel the truth in her words. She had not intended for this betrayal, it had all been her father's doing. And that Crosse bitch. He'd deal with her later.

"I'm not going anywhere," he said.

"But." She sniffed back the torrent, but the tears would not cease. "I—I need your heart."

"Then you shall have it." Michael tore open his shirt and dropped it to the fire. "Take my heart, Jane. It is yours."

"No," she whispered, the ax shaking in her hands.

"You must be quick," he said. "There isn't much time."

"No!" She tossed the ax to the ground between them. "How can you torture me like this? I love you, Michael!"

"Jane." He grabbed her by the shoulders. Everything faded into the background, the blaze, her father's expectant sneer, Isabelle's tiny moans from near the tree. Just they two stood alone, bonded by the magic they had given one another. "You can do this. *We* can do this. Take. The blood. From my heart."

"No—"

"And then bring me back."

Jane opened her mouth in a gape. "Wh-what?"

"Use your magic, Jane. Use *our* magic. The sex magic. It can work. I know it."

And if it did not?

The sacrifice was worth it.

"It can't—"

"It's worth a try. You have to." He picked up the ax and forced it into her loose grip, tightening his fingers around hers so she wouldn't drop it again. "Together, we are strong, Jane. Look into my eyes. Can't you see yourself? You already have my heart, now you've just to use it to save your life."

"You're not that strong, Michael. Maybe if you had my blood you could use real magic, but—"

"You must try, Jane!" Baptiste yelled.

Michael smirked at the father's eagerness. The old vampire had nothing to lose—save a daughter.

"I would rather die." Jane crossed her arms, steadfastly refusing Michael's attempts to wrap her fingers about the handle.

"Fine." Stepping back, he swung the ax in a full circle before him, like some ancient battle sword, and then swung it to hook in his grip against the curve of the blade. "I love you, Jane. Don't let me down. I want you around for eternity."

And he gouged the ax up into his chest. The tip burned through flesh. The sickening crunch of cartilage cracked.

Michael cried out. For the first time, his voice frightened the angels, and Heaven cringed. The bonfire consumed his cry.

He would not allow her to go through this alone. He'd ransomed his heart to her days ago. And he wasn't the sort of man to give things lightly—especially his heart.

Michael opened his mouth in a silent scream. It hurt like no sun ever could. But he did not stop, pressing the blade deeper into his body.

He fell to his knees.

A second died. A heartbeat broke in two. Jane's pulse severed from his own, leaving his body.

Blood spurt from his chest. Jane, all crimson and fire, knelt before him. Her mouth stretched open. But he couldn't hear her scream, only the drumbeat of his own manic heart.

Blood spattered Jane's face.

Michael smiled. This was the right thing to do. And if he didn't survive? Then he would go in peace knowing Jane would live.

"I just…wanted to give you life," he managed.

The bonfire crackled wickedly.

"I love you, Jane."

Chapter 25

"Michael? Can you hear me?"

An angel called to him. So distant. Fading, slipping away. Sounded familiar. And he'd thought he could never make it to heaven.

"Michael!"

"Hurry, J-Jane." Michael slapped his chest. Blood splattered his face. So much of his own blood. "Drink."

"No."

"Now! I did this for you. Don't let it be in vain!"

"Quickly, Jane," her father encouraged from somewhere Michael could not see. "Plunge your hand inside his chest. Take what you can."

Michael slapped his hand over Jane's and moved it to the hole in his chest. And then he blacked out.

* * *

"Is he dead?"

Jane heard her father's question, but she was too frantic to answer. Soaked with her lover's blood, she swiped at her face to clear her vision.

It was done. She'd completed the ritual.

And all she wished for now was her own death.

Baptiste knelt on the grass next to her and laid a hand over Michael's exposed chest beside Jane's trembling fingers. The ax had cleaved through flesh and cartilage, and had fitted itself between ribs. Jane could see bone.

"You did what was right," Baptiste said. "He wanted you to do it. You cannot blame yourself. Ever."

"Just tell me he'll live," she sobbed. "I don't want to live unless he does!"

"He may heal," Baptiste offered. "He is young. Strong. And if he has taken some of your magic…"

"Not enough," she said. "Never enough. He's staked himself! The heart is damaged."

Her father stuck a finger into the wound.

"What are you doing?" she shrieked.

"I can feel the heart. It's still beating. Though…"

"Your blood!" She gripped her father's wrist. "Please?"

Honeyied eyes darted between hers, reading her heart, knowing her as only he could know her. *Don't let me down, Daddy. Let this be the one you accept for your daughter.*

"Of course." Baptiste bit into his own wrist and Jane quickly pressed it over Michael's mouth.

"Is it working?"

"He is drinking. I can feel him draw it out," Baptiste said. He winced, and bowed his head over Michael. "Very much. But it won't be enough. I have not fed for weeks, Jane dearest."

And like that, Baptiste's wrist dropped way from Michael's mouth. Jane slapped his face gently. "Michael? Don't go. Please, I need you."

Baptiste spat into his palms. Once. Twice. And again. He slapped his hands together and rubbed.

Jane guessed his next move. Her father pressed his palms to Michael's chest. The vampire's saliva acted as a healing agent against a simple bite. Could it prove effective against a great hole cleaved into a man's heart?

Baptiste worked his fingers inside the wound, causing Jane to wince at the intrusion. She knew it was for the best, or at the very least, the only hope Michael had. He drew out his hands and spit on them again.

She wondered if there was enough magic in her arsenal to bring back a dying vampire. Likely not, unless it included a very involved spell and chanting and instructions from a grimoire that she did not have.

"How could I have done this? I've betrayed him. Daddy, I only wanted to love him. It was wrong, so wrong."

Her father's arms wrapped about her shoulders, but he didn't try to pull her away from Michael. Jane's fingers slid across his chest. Pressing her palm over the open wound didn't help, but the act of attempting to stop death—no, it didn't change a thing in her heart.

This night she had lost her heart with the swing of an ax.

"Move aside." Another woman's voice.

Jane frowned. She had forgotten all about the other. Michael had held her so covetously. He'd bowed his head over her and nudged his nose into her hair. Cherished. Witnessing them together had cut deeply into Jane.

Isabelle plunged to the ground between Jane and Baptiste and pushed aside Baptiste. The linen suit was smeared with dirt and blood. She looked a tattered angel.

She leaned over Michael, her long white hair dusting through the blood.

Now she saw how beautiful the woman was, even the scars that ravaged half her face danced delicately with the reflection of the flames. She didn't know what to say, so she said, "I'm so sorry."

"Get over it, witch. I saw the whole thing. He did this to himself. Obviously, because he loves you so much. The idiot." She surveyed Jane for a moment, her bloodshot gold eyes darting back and forth between Jane's. "Another witch. I cannot seem to get myself far enough away from your insane lot. And you call us the dark? You are wicked! And you," Isabelle addressed Baptiste, "a fellow of the blood?"

The female vampire shook her head and focused back on Michael. "I hope she's worth it, Michael. Now, sit back. Let me see what I can do."

Chapter 26

"Listen to me. Wake up. Don't die. You said you weren't going anywhere. Michael!"

The angel had returned. And this time she was angry.

A great whorl of fire burned in his chest.

Michael choked. Swallowed back blood. Sweet, rich liquid, laced with a familiar memory. Not his own. He'd taken blood? From whom?

"Michael? They've left. I made them go. We're alone. I'm not going to let you go. Michael!"

"J-Jane?"

What was that awful ache? And yet, more than being painful, it pulsed, tugging, almost as if it were cleaving together and making itself strong.

"Yes, listen to my voice, Michael. Concentrate. Try to find my heartbeats."

"Can't. You're not…there." He sighed a long breath, expelling streams of the unknown blood as well. "Whose blood…in my mouth?"

"Daddy's."

Her father had given him blood? Stunning.

"And Isabelle's."

Now that was even more remarkable. He couldn't be hearing right. The angel was wrong. He had descended to Hell where everyone lied and a vampire was forced to swim in the blood of others for eternity, always drowning, never living.

"She's safe now, Michael. My father took her back to town. But if you want me to have him bring her back to you, I will."

Isabelle LaPierre. The bloody mistress of his fate. La Belle Dame sans Merci, indeed.

Jane. Goddess of light.

There was no question who he had chosen.

"Michael?" Warmth traced his cheek. She touched him. He recognized that pulse.

"Isabelle," he murmured, for he couldn't find his voice yet. "Did she…take from me in return?"

"No."

Now there was a debt he could never live up to.

"Do you want me to bring her back?"

"Never. I love you, Jane."

"I'm so glad to hear that."

"Glad…to tell it."

"Then listen. You're still weak. Your chest has

closed up, but the damage within...well, I can't know how critical it is. Can you feel it? Gauge the wound?"

He shook his head, not wanting to do anything but listen to her voice. No matter what she said, the music of her danced him away from the pain inside. Light, yes, his Jane.

"We can do this," she said. "You're not going to die on me now."

"Jane. You're...alive?"

"So far. And so are you."

"No. I'm...dead. Can't...see."

"Open your eyes, lover. I'm going to kiss you," she offered.

Good. He liked Jane's kisses. What a way to go. Kissed by an angel— make that a witch who isn't really a witch, but maybe she is, and don't forget that vampire blood streaking through her system.

No, just plain Jane. That's who she was to him.

He felt her upon his mouth.

"Kiss me back, Michael!"

Something stung his cheek. She'd slapped him! Because she wanted him to focus...on...? Yes, the kiss. Her kiss. Kissing him because that is all he wanted in this world. There was a way back.

He'd no intention of leaving this world, so he'd better start the journey.

The kiss, yes, fall into it, answer her back with a kiss of his own. Hard, a little sloppy at first. *You know how to do this. Win her, seduce her, sing her into your veins.*

It felt good. Jane's mouth on his. Her breath pushing into him, flowing through him. Her heart beat inside him. In his heart? He couldn't know if it was wide open inside him, or if that tightening sensation were the organ closing up, healing—it had to be.

"Love you," she whispered. "Need you to stay here with me."

He kissed her back. And now he was able to lift his head and slide a hand behind her neck to keep her close. Never let her away. Keep the magic for himself.

This was right. Jane in his arms. Jane at his mouth.

He'd opened his heart for Jane. And now she stepped inside.

Rolling her onto her back, Michael leaned over Jane. The fire simmered close by, it had been reduced to ash. But not him—never ash. Nor her.

Yes, Jane's pulse had scampered back into his veins. He could feel her enter him, soaring through his blood and seeking his own pulse.

"Ah!" The pace of his own heart startled him so that he slapped a hand over his chest. Had it not been beating previously?

It was now. Like drums calling to the march. Jane resided there. And beneath him. She clung to his body and wrapped her legs about his hips.

"The sex magic," she said. "We must do it now, Michael. Take me."

Instinct moved him to his elbows. Jane unzipped his pants. A tug drew her skirt up above her hips. It all happened in *one, two, three* heartbeats. Thrusting into her, he cried out at the sweet agony of her heat. She surrounded him. She owned him. The magic seeped into him.

Jane cried out, and at the same time Michael surrendered to a thunderous climax. He continued to thrust into her, taking from her, giving to her. Sharing his dark with her light.

There was only one thing that could make his world right. One thing that would forever bind he and Jane for the eternity she had won this night beneath the wicked moon.

It was a risk. And he would take it.

Michael kissed Jane's mouth. Soft laughter invaded the tension. He loved that she laughed after orgasm.

In every way.

Drawing his lips across her mouth, he kissed a slow trail into the corner where her laughter opened the crease in a soft arc. Then, down her jaw, following the latent scent of lilacs, buried deep beneath the blood aroma, but there—it made him smile—the garden under his tongue.

Blood spotted her neck. His blood. He swiped it away with a lash of his tongue. Above, the wicked wild moon beamed down a spotlight upon the stage.

"Jane, thank you," Michael murmured against her neck.

"We did it," she said on an elated gasp. "You're alive."

"Alive, but not complete. Do you trust me?"

"Always."

As he leaned to Jane's neck the delicate ash and

floral smell of her flesh tempted Michael to kiss lightly the vein before tasting. He pulled away the soft strands of copper hair, slipping his fingers around the back of her head, and bit deeply, opening the vein in a hot gusher.

Jane moaned softly as the powerful sensations of blood release coursed through her body.

The blood moved swiftly through his body, tunneling through his veins at a speed so fast it was like a jolt of hot lightning. He could feel its passage as it tracked directly to his heart. His head filled with a wavering rhythm that pounded in his ears, vanquishing all other sounds that threatened to destroy the ecstasy.

No orgasm had ever been so all-encompassing and perfect. Jane shuddered uncontrollably in his arms.

Blood sex magic. Finally.

It was a long time before sounds started to fade in, as if a finger were being dragged slowly across a rotating record.

Things were becoming clearer, the swoon subsiding like sloe gin. He struggled to hold on to its last dizzying effects by hugging his arms tightly about Jane.

Clarity.

Unable to put words to the incredible high he had experienced, Michael closed his eyes. Trembling as he surrendered the last fleeting whispers of the swoon, he had the brief thought that this could be the beginning to the end.

Jane's blood could kill him—if Baptiste's blood had not made him immune to the witch's curse.

But he wanted to believe the father's blood had nothing to do with his life or death. No, this moment was entirely Jane and him. Together, they gave to each other what no one else could. Light and dark, and the entire universe in between.

Once again, Michael had become something different. And this different he could really embrace.

"Michael?"

He kissed the wounds on her neck, tracing his tongue over them to induce the healing. "I'm still here," he murmured. "We did it, Jane."

"Your heart?" She felt his chest, pressing tenderly. No pain. Even the inner ache had diffused. "Is it...?"

"Thanks," he said. "You did that. You healed my heart, Jane."

"Only because you gave it to me in the first place. So we really did it? You're feeling... strong?"

"I feel like I could fly."

"Wait a minute, vampire, even I can't fly."

"But with practice you could."

"True. So you think, with my blood, you can too?"

"I know so."

"Bewitched," she whispered aside his cheek. "You have become one of the bewitched now, Michael."

"In body, blood and soul, Jane. Bewitched by you, and happy to be so. You cold?"

"No." She looked about, pressed her hands to the

ground where they'd made love. "Are we going to have sex all night?"

"Until the sun rises."

"Sounds good, lover."

Chapter 27

A week later, they were buckled into the Mini, headed for California beneath the midnight sky. Eventually Michael had to return, get back to the band, and into the groove of life. And Jane did want to return to Venice, to tell her mother all about the magic she now possessed, and to begin her education in controlling it. But neither was in a rush.

Isabelle had left word with Baptiste to tell Michael that she believed Jane would be very good for him. She intended to seek another of her blood children, in hopes of healing her scars faster, and sent her love to Michael.

Baptiste had remained in town for a few days following the ritual, and visited Michael in town to say goodbye. "I was wrong about you," he said to Michael. "You are a fine young man. Even considering your propensity for distasteful, loud music. Take a look at the windows when you return to the house, will you?"

The windows had been installed yesterday afternoon, but Michael hadn't even looked at them, for he'd been too involved in Jane.

"There is such joy in the windows," Baptiste had said. "Nothing Jane has ever created has so screamed her happiness."

It was all about the scream. And the laughter that followed her gorgeous climaxes.

And so Michael had went home to look at the windows, Jane standing at his side, their hands clasped.

"Your father was right," he said. "They're gorgeous, and they absolutely scream joy." The vivid azure and emerald glass flowed into crimson and amber and violet. A dragonfly made its flight across the set of windows, landing on the head of a rock 'n' roll skull at the last window.

"It is how I feel inside," she'd said and hugged him tightly. "When I'm with you."

Now, with the car window rolled down and seat pushed as far back as possible, Michael propped one foot up on the doorframe and tapped the center console with his wrist, his bracelets jangling and keeping a steady beat.

"Oh, the wild wicked child of a witch," he sang.

Jane flashed him a smug grin.

"She's not a witch, just plain, plain Ja-ee-ane."

"Michael, stop."

"But that ole sex magic filled her up. And it gave her man a new habit."

"Oh, brother, that is so corny."

He ignored her obvious lack of musical appreciation, and sang on. "She gave me a black birthday cake—

"—and an ax through my heart, Oh, sweet Jane!"

He strummed the lick line out on his air guitar.

"Forever wild about my sweet Jaaaaane." He drew out her name in a long, twisting finale that would have made Jimmy Page proud.

With a wink, Michael asked, "Did you like that? I invoked the power of Led Zeppelin. Pretty damn cool if you ask me."

Jane stopped the car at a stop sign and leaned across the console, gripping Michael by the T-shirt. "Invoke this, rock star."

She kissed him there at the intersection that lead to their future, and a long one at that.

Life was good. In fact, life rocked.

nocturne™

WAS HE HER SAVIOR
OR HER NIGHTMARE?

HAUNTED
LISA CHILDS

Years ago, Ariel and her sisters were separated for
their own protection. Now the man who vowed
revenge on her family has resumed the hunt, and
Ariel must warn her sisters before it's too late.
The closer she comes to finding them, the more
secretive her fiancé becomes. Can she trust the man
she plans to spend eternity with? Or has he been
waiting for the perfect moment to destroy her?

On sale December 2006.

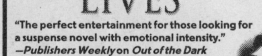